CRAMPS

SHARON   **MONIQUE**

VALERIE   **JANELLE**

DIANE

La Noyce Taylor

This is a work of fiction. Names, characters, businesses, places, events, locales, and incidents are either the products of the author's imagination or used in a fictitious manner. Any resemblance to actual persons, living or dead, or actual events is purely coincidental.

CLF Publishing, LLC.
www.clfpublishing.org
909.315.3161

Copyright © 2020 by La Noyce Taylor

Cover design by Senir Design. Contact information-info@senirdesign.com.

ISBN #978-1-945102-47-9

Printed in the United States of America.

Dedications

*This book is dedicated to my wonderful
niece Eshonna, who gave me the inspiration
to start this journey.*

Acknowledgements

I acknowledge my mother, may she rest in peace, who always told me to believe in myself and my goals in life. My children Christopher and Orlando whom the LORD blessed me to have the experience to birth and raise. I was so glad that the Lord was pleased to allow me to raise a handsome stepson Matthew since he was seven. My siblings Eusebio, Oletha, and my brother John, may he rest in peace, were with me from the very beginning. I love and cherish you. My daughter-in-law Deidra, whom I love very dearly. My sister-in-law Mary and Betsie, who have been there for a very long time. Much love to you and the remaining of my family, friends and loved ones. We're on beautiful journey. My extended family- a sister in Christ, Tina McDonald Moore, whom I call Thelma, a few co-workers Amanda, Nancy and Johnny, who believed in my dreams to help me get started with my book. Thanks so much for your love and support. A very special man in my life Virgil, who helped me very much with this book.

Finally, I would like to acknowledge my publisher, Dr. Cassundra White-Elliott, who was very instrumental in making this book become reality, and Deacon Charles and his mother, who I say the Lord used them as a Holy Ghost set up for me. I thank you all for everything. I love you very much.

I truly hope you will enjoy this novel, as there will be many more to come.

Chapter One

On a crisp winter morning, Valerie, at forty-three, is sitting at a corner table in a local coffee shop, working on her laptop. Although most people are there for the delicious, yet overpriced, coffee that is sold in a variety of flavors, Valerie is completely focused on finishing a proposal draft, as her deadline is rapidly approaching. In addition to the draft, she has a presentation to prepare. Meanwhile, orders are made, names are called, and orders are collected. During the hustle and bustle of the coffee shop, Valerie works hard to not lose her focus.

One table away from her, Gordon is set up to complete a little work himself. Just as he lays all needed materials out on the table, he realizes his laptop adapter cord is not long enough to be plugged into the outlet. He looks for a way to slide his table over, but he quickly realizes it is not feasible. What confounds matters is the only table that is near the outlet is already occupied. For a moment, Gordon takes in the beauty of the woman who is quietly and diligently working. He hates to disturb her. But at that moment, he really has no choice. He is up against a deadline.

Without causing a scene or startling the beautiful

woman, Gordon approaches her table. "Excuse me," Gordon begins in a soft voice.

"Yes?"

"Uh, hi."

"Hello," Valerie says cautiously, as his stunningly dreamy blue eyes catch her attention.

"I'm so sorry to bother you, but my laptop cord cannot reach the outlet from the table I'm sitting at," he said, gesturing to the nearby table. Valerie's eyes follow his gesture. "Would it be okay if I share your table with you?"

Feeling completely annoyed by his interruption, Valerie tries to mask her feelings by giving a hint of a smile. "Sure, that is fine," she answers, while immediately returning to her project. She wants to send the message that although she consented to him sitting at her table, she under no circum-stances wants to be disturbed.

Gordon begins to transfer his items from his table to Valerie's table. In the midst of the transfer, he pauses to introduce himself. "By the way, I'm Gordon," he says, exten-ding his hand for hers.

"Valerie," Valerie responds, barely lifting her head. When she sees his outstretched hand, she stops typing and offers him hers. As they shake, she notices his hand is strong and firm, while he notices the softness of hers.

Once the transfer from one table to the other is complete, Gordon decides he should put something in his stomach, so the growling that had begun a few minutes earlier would not disturb his focus. Before making his way to the counter, he asks Valerie, "Sorry to bother you, but can you watch my things while I grab something to eat? And, can I get you something as well?"

"No, thank you. I don't want anything."

Gordon goes to the counter and purchases a latte and two coffee cakes. When he returns to the table, he places one coffee cake next to Valerie's computer. She glances up, not knowing what to make of the gesture the handsome, blue-eyed man just made. So, she simply says, "You didn't have to do that."

"I know, but I wanted to, Mrs. Valerie," Gordon replies as he takes a seat and powers up his laptop, carefully sipping his latte.

"It's Ms. Valerie, not Mrs. I'm not married."

Taking note of her relationship status, Gordon continues to sip his latte while taking in the beautiful contours of her face. Valerie can feel his eyes on her, but she refrains from meeting his gaze. Well, at least for a while. A few moments later, she lifts the coffee cake to her lips and takes a small bite. As she does so, her eyes drift to the other side of the table as she takes in Gordon's sideburns and thick lips that are surrounded by his goatee.

For a while, they steal glances at each other while the other is seemingly unaware. But from time to time, their eyes meet. As the hour passes on, the stares they share become uncontrollable.

Chapter Two

In a luxurious corner office, of a sky rise building, planted in the heart of downtown, Diane Taylor is standing by the window, looking out at the skyline as she dictates to Danielle, her secretary, who is jotting down notes. Presently, Diane is one the top sales representatives at the call center, and she is always filled with creative ideas.

Appearing to be somewhere else entirely, Diane says, "I need the files on my desk by twelve, so I can prepare for my one o'clock meeting." Danielle does not bother to offer a verbal response, knowing by the look on her boss' face that she would not hear her. Danielle simply makes a gesture with her head, demonstrating her agreement.

Suddenly, Diane's pleasant but distant-looking facial expression shifts. She no longer looks melancholy; now, she appears to be in distress. Without a word, she lifts her left hand and begins to rub her lower stomach region. Danielle watches Diane closely. After a few moments pass, Danielle asks, "Is there anything else you need at the moment?" Diane slowly shakes her head. Danielle rises from her seat and makes her way back to the outer office to her desk, softly closing the door behind her.

Cramps

Later that morning, Diane is in the conference room. She is not feeling much better, but business must go on. Greeting the two men that are present, Diane puts on a bright smile and says, "Hello, gentlemen. I'm Ms. Taylor, but you can call me Diane. After going over all the material, I feel that this would make a great...." Instead of finishing her statement, she takes a deep breath to quell the stabbing pain that is shooting through her uterus. Then, she pauses an additional minute, acting as if she is deep in thought and trying to choose her words carefully. The reality is- her cramps are becoming increasingly stronger, nearly unbearable. Although she attempts to keep the look on her face pleasant and professional, her facial expressions slowly become more evil looking.

The men watch Diane carefully, wondering what has come over her and what direction the meeting is headed. One minute she was speaking calmly to them, seemingly excited about their proposal. In the next minute, she seemed to have mentally left the room. Before they can ask a question, Diane abruptly says, "I need to brainstorm for a minute. Talk between yourselves for a moment. As a matter of fact everything sounds good." As Diane darts from the room, both men look questioningly at each other, wondering what ideas Diane was referring to because they had not yet engaged in a conversation.

Diane had conjured up a quick plan to leave the room, catch her breath, allow the pain to pass, and resume the meeting. But, the stabbing is growing more and more severe. She realizes she will be unable to stand or sit still for the duration of the meeting, so she knows it is better to go to Plan C. Re-entering the room, Diane's next statement confounds the situation even further. Looking directly at the two men, Diane says, "Something just came up. I'll schedule another meeting for this project next week. Have a great day." Almost running from the room, Diane makes her way quickly to the ladies' room, leaving her guests to leave the building on their own.

About an hour later, having taken a couple of Midol, Diane makes her way from her office to the group of cubicle that fills the inner sanctum of the call center. Diane is heading to speak with Vanessa, one of the ladies in the office. Just as she makes her way to Vanessa's cubicle, a loud buzzer goes off! The sound is deafening to Diane's ears. She is already on edge because of her hormones being out of whack, and the loud buzzing that is penetrating her eardrums is not helping. Lifting her head and looking around anxiously, Diane says, "What the hell! What's that noise?"

Before anyone can answer, another voice calls out. Having gained everyone's attention in the office, Mr. Daniel Thomas, the department supervisor, requests for all employees to come over to where he stands, which is the southeast corner of the sales floor. He is everyone's boss, even Diane's. As everyone begins to walk over to Mr. Thomas, others begin to inquire about the wretched sound as well. Making her way with her coworkers, Vanessa asks, "What is that?" as the noise rings through their workspace again. Confused, everyone wears a frown upon their face. Everyone except Mr. Thomas. With a huge grin spread across his face, Mr. Thomas answers everyone's question: "It's a punch clock along with an alarm. It is something new that we are trying out. It's going to sound off on every break, including lunch and afternoon break, and also at the end of your shift."

Keisha, another sales rep, retorts, "For years, we've been doing just fine signing in and out from our computers. Why the change now?"

Looking around at everyone, Mr. Thomas responds, "It's for a better tracking system for this department.

Hearing his response, Diane throws her hand on her hip, waves a finger on her other hand, and replies, "Well, that right there is not the business! I don't need to be tracked." Her response catches everyone's attention, including Mr. Thomas'. Most of them are appalled by her outburst, but they are not surprised at all. She is well known for making outbursts such as that.

Leah chimes in and taps Diane on the arm. "Girl, calm down!" She gives Diane the warning because she would hate to see anyone lose her job for voicing her opinion.

Catching herself, Diane lowers her voice to a whisper and tells Leah, "Hum, child.... He's trying to raise my blood pressure!" Leah gets a chuckle out of that.

Seeing that his new idea is being met with resistance, Mr. Thomas attempts to encourage his employees that his new gadget is a splendid idea. Keeping a cheery disposition, he says, "Give it a try. You'll see. I think you will like it."

Eventually, everyone goes back to their respective work stations, shaking their heads as they go. At every break, the annoying alarm sounds off. Everyone feels frustrated, especially Diane. Before the second afternoon break, the punch clock with the alarm goes missing. In its place are some donuts along with a sign saying: "Have a nice day!"

After lunch, Mr. Thomas comes back to the office early to see how the alarm is working out. Seeing the sign and no machine, he exclaims, "It's missing! Where is the machine?" Looking frantically about, Mr. Thomas surveys the room. All he sees is innocent-looking faces and a box of donuts. Finally, he steps over to the box, grabs a donut, turns back to his employees, and says, "Y'all just ghetto!" Stuffing the donut in his mouth, he angrily walks back to his office. This time, he is the one shaking his head.

Chapter Three

On a warm, sunny afternoon, Rodney stops by Monique's home for a visit. She has not seen him in a few days, so she takes his visit as a nice opportunity for an outing even though she isn't feeling her best. He consents, and she opts for the movies. She is excited that he agrees without hesitation. Sometimes, he gives her a hard time and insists they spend a quiet evening indoors. Happily, Monique follows Rodney outside, as they head to his car. On the ride, they make small talk as they make their way to the theater, which is only a few blocks away.

Once they arrive to the theater, Rodney purchases the tickets; then, he escorts his girlfriend inside. Finding the perfect location to sit, not directly under the air conditioning vent, but in the middle of the row and directly in front of the screen, Monique sits down. Before Rodney can get too comfortable, Monique asks, "Rod, can you go get me some popcorn?"

Wanting to please her and keep their evening out going smoothly, Rodney answers, "Sure, anything else?"

"Chocolate candy sounds nice," Monique says with a smile, noticing her man's pleasant mood.

"What kind?"

"It doesn't make a difference."

Rodney makes his way back out to the lobby to purchase the requested items. Meanwhile, Monique sits in her seat anticipating the movie. She has wanted to see it since it first came out, but this is the first chance she has had to do so. When Rodney re-enters the theatre, he looks through the semi-darkness for the top of Monique's head to find her exact location. At first, he doesn't see her. She appears to be bending down towards the floor. By the time, he reaches her, he sees she is holding her stomach and letting out slow moans and groans.

"Are you okay?" he inquires.

Not wanting to change his mood due to her personal situation, she sits up straight and answers, "I'm fine."

He questions the truthfulness of her answer, but the movie starts, so he lets it go and takes his seat, handing her the treats. As the movie continues, Rodney doesn't think anything else about the brief conversation. Monique, on the other hand, continues to massage her stomach in the darkness.

Once the movie ends, Rodney and Monique leave and head back towards her home in silence. A few minutes later, Monique breaks the quiet that surrounds them, by asking, "Can we stop by the store for a hot second?"

"For what? To get some wine or something?" Rodney asks, feeling anxious as he anticipates a positive outcome for the night.

"Nope! But, I do need to get something else though."

With a questioning look on his face, Rodney asks, "Well, what is it? What do you need to get?" He wonders why she isn't her normal direct self. The look on her face tells him he may not want to know the answer.

Hesitantly, Monique says, "I really don't think you want to know. I'll put it this way, my friend came to hang out with me for a week."

The look that suddenly covers Rodney's face is no surprise to Monique. She really hated to tell him because she knew his whole demeanor would change. And, she was correct. A scowl covers his face when he asks, "What! Are you serious! Why now?" His question sounds as if though he has wasted his entire evening by taking her out only to be disappointed in the end because what he had anticipated happening was not going to.

By now, Monique can no longer hold her frustration, so instead of answering calmly, she spurts out, "What do you mean 'why now'! I don't have any control over that, fool! Just take me home!"

Without saying another word, Rodney punches the gas and heads toward Monique's home as if he cannot get there fast enough. Upon their arrival, Rodney pulls up to the curb without any intention of getting out. He knows Monique is pissed, and he isn't in the best of moods either. When she opens the car door, he says, "I'll check you out in a week!" Not having the words to fully express her disappointment in him, she gives him a cruel look and exits the vehicle in a huff.

Chapter Four

Sitting at home in her beautifully decorated dining room, Valerie is at the table with her attention trained on her laptop. Just as she decides to check her email, a new one comes in. Clicking it open, she sees it is from Gordon, her new 'friend' from the coffee shop that she had met just that morning.

"Valerie, what are you doing besides working on your laptop?" his email reads.

Valerie smiles, as she reads his assuming question. "How do you know I'm working? I could be doing something else."

"Look how fast you replied. Timing is everything," Gordon replies.

Valerie laughs at his response, as she types, "So, what's up, Gordon?"

While she awaits his next witty reply, she walks into the kitchen for a cup of coffee. Smelling the sweet yet strong aroma, she pours herself a cup and returns to her laptop, hoping to see another email from Gordon.

Gordon is at his home in the living room as well. Only he is at his coffee table, sipping a smooth glass of wine.

Continuing their email banter, he writes, "I have a question for you."

Without hesitation, Valerie responds, "I'm listening," as she wonders where the conversation is going. Because she had just met him, she has no idea where his mind is or what his intentions are towards her. But, she is definitely interested in finding out. While Valerie is wondering about the handsome man on the other end of the computer connection, his question comes in.

"So, how is it that a beautiful woman like yourself is not married or involved with someone?"

Seeing where the conversation is headed, Valerie goes along with his direction. "I was involved with this guy for a couple of years until I found out that he met a female online. He left me for her. I haven't seen or heard from him since." Valerie didn't really want to go into the conversation, but she felt comfortable discussing it behind the shelter of the computer screen.

Her response peeked Gordon's curiosity, causing him to ask, "How long has it been since that happened?"

"Around five or six months now." Then, turning the focus away from her, she inquired about his romantic life, without waiting for his response to her last answer. "What about you? Why don't you have a special someone in your life?"

"I went through something similar. I was with a woman for close to a year; then, I found out she was cheating on me. I let her go because I didn't want to be with someone who wanted to be with me and someone else." Gordon began to reminisce about his past relationship, while looking out the window. Quickly, he decided to let it pass and look toward the future. So, he wrote, "Come off that computer. Let's go and have some fun."

Although she was amenable to the open conversation, she had not anticipated the invitation. "I just met you today. I don't know anything about you nor do you know anything about me." She was really unsure about his invitation. She didn't know what to make of it. She was accustomed to taking precautions when it came to dating. Interrupting her thoughts, another email came through.

"What would you like to know? Just ask, and I will tell you. I'm not trying to hurt you. I just want to get to know you better. Just want to have some fun for a change. Nothing serious just fun. So, how about it?"

As she reads his words, she wants to believe in their innocence, but she can't help to question his intentions. "So, where are you talking about going?"

Becoming hopeful at the prospect of seeing her again, he grins as he types, "It's a surprise."

Chapter Five

Having finally ended her work day, Diane is home relaxing in her family room. The pains she was experiencing earlier are continuing to annoy her. Trying to find a comfortable position, she lies down on the couch, then the recliner, next the sofa bed… To her dismay, she cannot find comfort anywhere. Finally, she walks into the master bedroom and into her well-used bathroom. Opening the medicine cabinet, she reaches for the Midol and quickly downs a couple of the pills.

As she waits for the Midol to kick in, she lies down on the bedroom floor with her legs uplifted on the bed. As time goes on, she drifts off to sleep only to be awakened by stabbing pains in her abdomen. So, back to the bathroom she goes to retrieve more pills. Suddenly, the lights go out!

"What the hell!" Diane exclaims. "This doesn't make no damn sense! How am I supposed to suffer in the dark? Let there be light!" Then, she thought to herself, *What am I doing? I'm not God.*

To help relieve the situation of being surrounded by darkness, she goes to the kitchen and retrieves a candle from the drawer and lights it. Returning to her room, she begins to pray, "Lord, I need help in a real way!" After placing the candle on her night table, she again lies on the floor, as she continues to pray. "Lord, I'm lying here in the dark in agony! Can you please send me a miracle? Or, at least can you please shorten this week? This is a hot mess! I need new furniture, a bed, a car, and most of all, I need light! In Jesus' name, I pray. Amen." Then, she opens her eyes.

As if though she is surprised to see the outcome of her prayer or the lack thereof, she yells, "Lord, I'm still in the dark! I just prayed to you! Can you help a sistah out? I know you're busy! But, the rest of the world has light!" Then, to see how far the devastation runs, she picks up the remote and attempts to turn on the television. When a picture fails to appear, she screams out, "I don't have no electricity! I'm 'bout to have a fit up in here!"

Chapter Six

Walking through the Los Angeles Airport, Rodney finds it hard to concentrate on his job. Instead, he is thinking about his lost opportunity with Monique. Seemingly out of nowhere, an idea comes to him. *Maybe all is not lost*, he thinks. *I can call my girlfriend Sharon and see what she's up to.* Pulling out his cell phone, Rodney dials Sharon's number. Sharon has just ended her shift at the hospital, where she works as a registered nurse. In the parking garage, as she makes her way to her car, her cell phone rings. Seeing her boyfriend's phone number, she answers with a smile that reaches from one ear to the other.

"Hey, honey," she greets Rodney.

"What's up, Sharon? How you doin', baby?"

"I'm fine. I'm just leaving work, heading to my car. What are you doing?"

"You know, I'm still on the grind. Taking a short break right now. But, I'll be getting off soon. How about we hook up? How about you get all dolled up and come over and hang out with me for a little while?"

Rodney's words stop Sharon in her tracks. His words are making her tingle. "Well, I am kinda of tired, but hearing your voice makes me up for anything."

Rodney likes the way Sharon is responding to his invitation. He feels like his luck just might change. So, he locates a bench that is against the wall, and he sits down and talks to her. "Anything?" he asks, to be sure they are on the same page. In the semi-darkness, in a corner of the dock, Rodney awaits Sharon's response. But, Sharon doesn't respond right away because she is digging through her purse attempting to locate her car keys. Rodney repeats himself, growing impatient. Interrupting his question that comes a second time, Sharon answers, "Hey, I know what we can do. Let's catch a late movie."

"Oh, no!" Rodney protests, as he stands up from the bench. "Nah, I'm all movie'd out!"

His response catches Sharon off guard. "All movie'd out? We haven't been in a while. So, what are you talking about?"

Catching his slip of the tongue, Rodney responds, "Umm… I'm talking about the movies on cable. You know... I watch those all the time." *Good save,* he praises himself mentally.

"Hummm…, you sound suspect," Sharon says, as she laughs and teases her man. "Alright, give me about an hour or so."

Rodney perks up at her response. "Alright, baby. I'll see you in an hour." After ending the call, Rodney goes back to work to finish up the last part of his shift. As he walks back over to his designated work station and pulls his work gloves on, he says to himself, "Now that's what I'm talking about. That's why it's always good to have one in the wings. Yeah!"

After Sharon arrives home, she quickly undresses and turns off the light, needing a moment of rest before her evening with Rodney. She walks over to her plush bed and sits on the edge. Out of the blue, knots become entangled in her stomach. Slowly, she leans over and lies down. Slowly, she begins to understand the discomfort she had been feeling in her lower back and her fatigue throughout the day.

Meanwhile, Rodney makes it home from work. He immediately begins to prepare for his night with his queen. He wants to ensure he is good and ready when she arrives. After showering, he stands in the bathroom, wearing nothing but a towel around his waist. In the mirror, he surveys himself thoroughly and notices his nose hairs could use a trim. "Let the grooming process begin," he says, as he reaches for the nose clippers. After his face is in top form, he checks out his irresistible six pack as he flexes. He is so taken with himself that he kisses his right muscle and then the left one. Finally, to complete the package, he dashes on cologne.

In his bedroom, Rodney pulls out a debonair ensemble. After adorning himself, he looks in his full-length mirror, impressed with what he sees. He knows Sharon always appreciates his taste in clothes, and he does not want anything to spoil their mood for the evening. One disappointment for the day is all he can handle.

Sharon awakens from her power nap, but she feels groggy. *This night is a wrap. I do not feel like moving even an inch,* she thinks. Cutting off her thoughts is the buzzing of her cell phone. "Hello...," she answers, glancing at the clock over the dresser.

Holding the phone in one hand, Rodney dims the lights with his other hand. "Hey, baby. Where you at? I just put the final touches on, so we can have a beautiful evening together. Why do you sound like you just woke up?"

Trying to shake the groggy feeling away, Sharon slowly moves her head from side to side. "Because I did. Sorry, boo. But me coming over tonight is not going to happen. There has been a change!" Sharon lets out a long sigh, as she lifts herself from the bed to go to the medicine cabinet to find something to relieve her discomfort.

Hearing his girlfriend's words, Rodney wants to throw his phone against a wall. "Change? What change? Baby, don't do this to me tonight. Is there something you need? Gas? More time to get ready? Just tell Big Daddy what it is, and I got you!" There was desperation in his voice, as he tried to salvage the evening that was already going downhill.

"No, babe. It's not any of those, but say 'hello' to my little friend! My cycle came around to see me for a week."

"Not again!" Rodney yelled.

Sitting on the bed with a bottle of Pamprin in her hand, Sharon's back straightens, and her attitude begins to flare up. "This is my first time telling you about this. What do you mean 'not again.' Who have you been talkin' to?"

24

Rodney, in his frustration, responds, "Nobody! You trippin'. I'll holla back at you later. Much later!" Without another word, he disconnects the call. The loving guy that was speaking to his woman a minute ago was out the window. He had been replaced with his true self- the self-centered man he really was. Fuming, Rodney paces the floor wondering how his luck could have turned out so badly- all in one day. "Damn! I can't believe this! I must be slippin' about their timing!" He just shook his head in wonderment, as he fell down into a sitting position on the sofa and let his head rest against the back.

Chapter Seven

The surprise Gordon has for Valerie is a candlelight dinner onboard his royal green extravagant double-deck yacht. As they stand along the side of the yacht in the moonlight, enjoying the scenery, Valerie looks directly at Gordon and asks, "Whose yacht is this?"

Not losing his smile for even a moment, Gordon casually answers, "It's mine. I recently purchased it. How do you like it?"

Blushing and slightly embarrassed for being so forward, Valerie compliments the yacht. "It's beautiful." Then, she shifts her attention from her surroundings to the décor on the table. She takes in the candlelight arrangement Gordon had his staff prepare for the two of them. Quietly, a servant walks over to the table and pulls out a chair, gesturing for her to come and take a seat. Valerie follows the command, as Gordon takes the seat across from her.

As they enjoy their dinner, music softly plays as a light breeze blows around them. The dinner consists of baked salmon, red roasted potatoes, broccoli, Cesar salad, and lightly buttered dinner rolls, and it melts upon their tongues, as they share light conversation and get to know each other better. After finishing their last bites of food, they wash it all down with a glass of the smoothest wine Valerie has ever consumed.

Looking at her with tender eyes, Gordon asks, "Would you like to go up on the deck?"

Unable to resist, Valerie gives a one-word consent, as she lifts herself from the seat, "Sure." Before she can fully rise to her feet, Gordon is behind her, assisting her with her chair. "Thank you," she says in almost a whisper.

Standing at the rail and looking into the moonlit water, Gordon continues to field questions to Valerie, to continue to break the ice and make her comfortable. "So, how long have you been working at that insurance company?"

"It's been ten years. How about you? How long have you been slaving away at your father's law firm?" she asks with a smile on her face, to let him know she is just teasing.

"Eleven years next week."

"Congratulations!"

"Thanks. I love it there. The passion of winning my cases gives me such a thrill, a true rush. It's surreal. To me, I feel as though I was born to do this. I cannot imagine myself doing anything else. And, I count it to truly be a blessing."

"I know what you mean. Not everyone is blessed to be able to do something they love or have a passion for."

"True that," Gordon agrees.

"After my failed relationship, I kinda plunged myself into my career and never looked back. I know that job like I know the back of my hand. But, taking a break is always good, too. Coming out tonight was such a treat. Thank you for the invitation, and thank you for dinner."

"And, what about the company?" Gordon inquires.

"The company is just as intriguing," Valerie answers blushing. To keep Gordon focused and not moving too quickly, she quickly changes the direction of the conversation. Looking away from him, she asks, "So, tell me. What's the name of your boat?"

"I haven't chosen one yet." He pauses for a moment. Then, he asks, "If this were your yacht, what would you name it?"

"I really have no idea."

"How about 'Lovely Val'?"

Surprised, Valerie shakes her head in disagreement. "No..."

"Okay. How about 'My Valerie'?"

"Really? You don't even know me that well."

"But, I'm getting to know you, and I like what I have seen up to this point. So far, we have shared a table together, emails, and dinner."

Valerie cannot believe the words Gordon is saying and with such ease. She just smiles and shakes her head, taking in all the attention he is showing. Meanwhile, she notices they are approaching land, and the boat docks. Not really expecting to have been going anywhere in particular, she is a little caught off guard. Not wanting to show concern, she casually asks, "Where are we?"

"Catalina Island."

Letting her concern grown into excitement, she says,

"This is nice! I have never been to Catalina Island."

Surprised at her response, Gordon asks, "Really? Are you enjoying yourself?"

Looking out at the land, Valerie exclaims, "Yes, this is so beautiful. I'm having a great time. Because you did all of this, I would like to do something for you if you are not too busy on Friday evening, say around seven?"

Gordon's heart beams with pride, with the realization he did something to make her smile. In turn, a huge smile covers his face. "For you, my calendar has just become cleared."

Valerie blushes at his response, and the moonlight hits her cheeks, showing their natural glow.

Chapter Eight

On Tuesday morning, instead of making her way to work at her regularly scheduled time, Diane decides to visit a furniture store because she cannot deal with her same old bed that has been needing replacing for quite a while. Although she is attending to her personal needs, she doesn't shirk *all* professional responsibilities. Before she browses the showroom floor, she takes out her cell phone and calls her job. When someone answers, Diane immediately engages the person in quick conversation. "Hello? What you doin'? Yeah. Look, tell your boss, I'm going to be late comin' in." Walking up to a king size bed, she disconnects the call without a word of goodbye.

Her presence captures the attention of Ralph, one of the store clerks. He looks her over carefully and believes he may have the chance of making a great sale on a king size bed. "Good morning. May I help you with something specific today?" Ralph asks Diane in his best cheerful tone.

Diane is not nearly as cheerful as Ralph. She looks him up and down, while responding, "Yeah! Can you get me a blanket, a sheet, and some hot tea? Oh, and do you have any relaxing and healing music? Something that sounds like water or the ocean perhaps?" As she names off the items, she taps a finger from one hand onto the fingers of her other hand, as though she is making a list.

Ralph looks at Diane in bewilderment, wondering why he had to be the one to get stuck with her. "What the…?" he exclaims. "Uh, ma'am. This is a furniture store! We sell beds, couches, and chairs! Oh, my…" he said, clutching his pearls. Softly to himself, he whispers, "This is going to be a hot mess!"

Continuing to be rude and sarcastic, Diane yells, "Then, why are you over here harassing me? Poof be gone!" Diane waves her hand as though it is a magical wand.

Feeling quite embarrassed, as the other customers stop to pay attention to the spectacle Diane is creating, Ralph walks away. He makes himself busy in another part of the store.

Not much later, Ralph is making his way from one section to another, cleaning as he goes. He wants to keep the store presentable for all potential customers. As he nears the section of reclining chairs, he spots Diane in a recliner. To his amazement, she is upside down! He hears her say, "Oh, Lord!" He wants to question her about her behavior and how she is treating furniture that does not belong to her. Remembering her nasty attitude a few moments earlier, he decides to walk away and ignore her.

Just as he turns around, Diane snaps, "Excuse me!"

Under his breath, Ralph says, "Here we go again." To Diane, he says, "Yes?"

"What is your turn around time?" Diane inquires.

Again, under his breath, Ralph whispers, "You need to turn around and walk right out this store." Audibly, he asks, "Turn-around time for what?"

Displaying much attitude, Diane answers, "I want the bed I was lying on- king size -with this recliner," as she gestures to the chair. "So, how long will it take for you to have it delivered to my house and remove the bed that's there?" Before Ralph can answer, Diane reaches into her pocket and grabs her keys. Thrusting them towards Ralph, she says, "I don't have time for this. Take my keys! My address is 1329 W. First Street. I'll meet you at the house in a few hours. I have to go to Walmart and purchase some pillows since you don't sell them here!"

Really fed up with Diane's attitude, Ralph loses all professionalism and matches her tone. "Lady! I can't take your keys nor can anything be removed unless you are there!"

"Look, Barney!" shouts Diane.

"It's Ralph!" he yells back.

"W-h-a-t-e-v-e-r!" she says, dragging the word out. "I don't like your attitude. Once again, why are you here harassing me? Didn't I tell you once before to leave me alone? You know what? I'm going over to Sears, where I can be treated with respect!"

Ralph thinks about walking over to the door and opening it for her. Instead, he says, while pointing, "It's two lights down. Then, make a left. You can't miss it!"

Appalled at his attitude towards her, Diane yells, "Don't

get beat down today! The way I'm feeling right now, I will knock you out!" Making her way to the door, Diane throws her hand in Ralph's face as she passes by him.

Chapter Nine

Enjoying the warm afternoon, Rodney hangs out with a few of his friends on the basketball court. He has not seen them in a while, so he enjoys himself as they run up and down the court. Plus, he needs the exercise, so he is trying to break a sweat. Work has been keeping him busy, so he is feeling a little sluggish.

After a couple games of basketball, Rodney notices his mind isn't really in the game. *I thought ballin' would help my pent-up frustration*, he thinks. He is still pretty pissed about how yesterday afternoon and last night went. He struck out twice. *Well, I have one more shot at getting lucky*, he thinks. He decides to give his last girlfriend Janelle a call to see if her schedule has any room for him. He takes a break between games and rings her phone.

Janelle is a waitress at Denny's. She has been taking orders and talking to customers since her shift began late that morning. Just as she heads to the breakroom to take her twenty-minute break, to give her feet a little rest, she feels her cell phone vibrating in her apron pocket. Softly, she answers, "Hello?"

"What's up, sweetheart?" Rodney greets her, hoping

she is in a splendid mood.

"Missing you that's all. How you doin'? I haven't heard from you in a while. Where have you been?"

Rodney knew Janelle was going to say something about how long it's been since they last spoke. All his women have the same conversation. But, he decides to let it pass and focuses on keeping the conversation light. "Working for that dolla! Right now, I'm just hanging out with my boys, shooting some ball. As far as you and I are concerned, we need to make up for lost time." Before going any further, Rodney decides it's best to dig a little deeper before making definite plans. "Wait a minute! How are you feeling? Any cramps or anything?"

Janelle cannot believe her ears. His words excite her. "OMG! How did you know? I knew we had a spiritual connection, and for you to know my cycle timing, I love you so much right now."

Rodney is not trying to hear all the lovely-dovey stuff at that moment. Her words just got to the heart of the matter, and he doesn't have time for it. Not able to hide his disappointment, he yells, "Damn!" as he starts to pace around the court. Quickly, he disconnects the call without another word.

Janelle is confused by Rodney's response and how he simply dismissed her that way. In her mind, it really is not like him. Looking at the time on her phone, she sees it is time for her to go back to work, but she decides to call him back to see what his issue is. Instead of getting him on the line, she reaches his voicemail, which says, "I know you're sorry you missed me. Leave your name and number. I'll hit those digits back." Irritated that she is now talking to a machine, she leaves an irate message. "Why the hell you hang up? I thought you loved me, punk!" Leaving the message does nothing to cool her down, so she dials his number again.

Holding his phone in his hand, he looks at the screen as Janelle's number shows up over and over again. He is extremely pissed and wonders why he can't get a break with any of his women. Knowing Janelle is not going to stop calling, he finally answers. "Hello."

Janelle does not hold back. She completely loses it. "You knew I was calling you back. Why didn't you answer? Oh, and you hung up in my face, too?"

Rodney tries to appease her by saying, "I didn't hang up, baby. My phone died! I'm about to go back and finish up this game. I'll check you out later!"

Knowing his phone had not died and suddenly come back to life that quickly, she yells, "I soooo don't believe you, but whatever!" She hangs up on him, as she fumes and goes into the ladies' room, so she can collect herself before returning to the restaurant floor.

Rodney is trying to keep the drama to a minimum, but his boys are getting wind of it anyway. They see the look that covers his face. One of them says, "Man, you look stressed! Did you get fired or something?"

Rodney does not want to get into the details with them, so he says, "Naw, man. I gotta go! I'll check y'all out later." Rodney makes his exit, wondering how he is going to smooth things over with Janelle later. But for now, he is not too concerned.

Chapter Ten

Later that afternoon, the day is still sunny and bright, and Valerie sits in her office with a warm feeling in her belly. She feels alive again. She has really taken a liking to Gordon. Leaning back in her chair, she begins to reminisce about the short time they have known each other when she hears a knock on her door. "Come in," she says.

A delivery man enters, bringing a dozen long-stemmed red roses. Knowing immediately who they are from, her smile grows brighter. Valerie stands up from her desk and accepts the delivery as she thanks the delivery man. As he turns and walks away, not leaving Valerie time to give him a tip, Valerie removes the card, which reads, "Just for you, 'my Valerie'." She blushes, and her heart leaps, as she leans over to take in the sweet aroma that only roses can emit.

While Valerie sits at her desk daydreaming, in an office bathroom at a law firm, Gordon has love written all over his face. He knows Valerie should have received the delivery by now. He wonders if she likes the roses. He is looking forward to seeing her later that evening, but for now, he has to finish his day before heading home. He splashes water on his face to help him focus on his cases before returning to his desk.

Later that evening at 7pm, a stretch limousine pulls up in front of Gordon's house. Valerie sits quietly as she awaits Gordon's arrival inside the car. Five minutes later, his front door opens, and he steps out looking more handsome than she has ever seen him looking, although he is dressed casually, as she instructed him. Once inside the limo, Gordon slides over next to her and plants a gentle kiss on her lips. He is impressed by Valerie's sense of class and what she has done to make the night special thus far. Looking around the plush vehicle, he nods and says, "So, I see you're full of surprises, also." He allows his eyes to fall over Valerie's entire body, focusing mainly on the fitted Levi jeans she is wearing. "You look beautiful as always."

Blushing profusely, she says, "Thank you. You look nice yourself."

Glancing down at his own ensemble, he says, "Thanks. Now for the big question. Where are we going?"

Not wanting to give anything away, she says coyly, "You'll see. I hope you like it." As she speaks, she hopes her plans are not off target and that he truly enjoys the evening.

Having no idea of what to expect, he says, "I love it already." His main focus is not where they are going, but with whom he is spending the evening. She has truly made his evening. He enjoys being in her company.

Moments later, the limo pulls into the Staples Center, in the Special Parking area. Gordon's excitement grows, and it can be readily seen on his face. After parking, the chauffeur opens the door for them. With light steps, they walk into the foyer of the Staples Center holding hands. "This is cool. I didn't know you like basketball."

"I do very much. I love the Lakers. I watch a little football, too. But, I'm not into other sports though."

Taking in Valerie's words, Gordon grows more excited. "That's cool! You don't find too many women into sports at all. They just tolerate it for their significant other." Valerie nods in agreement to what Gordon is saying, as she takes out her pass, so they can enter.

Instead of going to the bleachers like all the other fans, Valerie guides Gordon to the elevators and into a private room. He didn't think he could be any more impressed after riding in the limo and arriving at the Staples Center. But, Valerie had not failed when she put together an awesome evening for the two of them. And, he is appreciating every moment of it. Giving her a hug, he surveys the suite. "I have been to multiple games here at the Center but never in a private room. This is really nice."

"I have a season pass for this room right here. For some games though, I am not going to be able to make it. But if you want, you can bring a few of your friends and enjoy yourselves. My treat."

"Wow, Val. Not only are you beautiful but very thoughtful. When I first met you, I was very attracted to you. And... I hope this doesn't bother you for me to say this to you: I love you, Valerie Hamilton."

Taking a deep breath, experiencing a little shock from

Gordon's statement, Valerie says, "I don't know what to say. In the beginning, we only shared a table. Then, my feelings started to grow the more time we spent together. I haven't felt this way, well… in a very long time. I love you too, Gordon Benson."

As their shared embrace lingers on, a cheer erupts from the fans, nearly startling them. Realizing the game has started, they move toward the food that is lining an eight-foot table. They fill their plates with sandwiches, hot wings, fresh fruit, chips, salsa, and cheesy bread. Eventually, they turn their attention to the game and enjoy themselves, as they cheer the Lakers on.

Chapter Eleven

Inside Walmart, Diane is walking through the store, looking for a few household items. Quite unexpectedly, she sees her three nieces, who are also walking throughout the store. Before she can approach them, all of a sudden, they go in three different directions, each one grabbing her stomach. From what Diane can see, they all start cramping at the same time. *Why is that?* she wonders. Before she can call even one of their names, she can see that their emotions are out of control.

Surprisingly, one niece lies down under a clothes rack with a pillow she pulled from their shopping cart and a coat she pulled off a rack that she is now using to keep her body warm. Within those few minutes, her body temperature dropped. It is as though she is trying to shut the world out while being right in the midst of it. As she tries to comfort herself, small whimpers escape her mouth, and tears run down her cheeks.

Another one of Diane's nieces walks into a dressing room, with no clothes to try on. She only wants a quiet place to lie down. She can't take the bright lights that are positioned around the store. They seem to be stabbing her in her eyes. She lies down on the floor inside one of the dressing rooms and closes her eyes. Unfortunately, the dressing room does nothing to alleviate her pain, so she desperately searches for something else because the pain is growing more and more severe by the moment. She climbs on top of a glass jewelry case and positions her knees upward, trying to give her stomach a little relief. She pays no attention to the people who walk by wondering if she has lost her mind. Diane grows irritated at the looky-loo's and issues a directive, "Keep it moving! Nothing to see here!"

Meanwhile, their sister, Diane's third niece, is attempting to find comfort as well. Her choice seems the most unlikely of them all and the most dangerous. She climbs on top of a conveyor belt, at an empty check stand, and folds herself into the fetus position. Watching them, Diane understands their physical pain and emotional torment. Her desire is for them to have comfort and understanding. Looking around, Diane notices her nieces are not the only ones in pain. There is a Chinese woman who is sitting on a bench, mumbling to herself in Chinese. At first, Diane thinks maybe the woman is the one who has lost her mind... until she sees the woman holding her stomach. That single gesture lets Diane know exactly what the woman's problem is.

"Damn! Damn! Damn! I can't stand this," the woman says in English, as she stands up from the bench and walks away, taking one tender step at a time.

Not having much else to do and not being able to comfort her nieces, Diane stands idly looking around the store. There is movement that catches her attention. Down the medicine aisle, there is a white woman with a shopping cart. She is literally pulling all the Midol and Pamprin from the shelves into her shopping cart. "Wow, she is stocking up! I don't blame her," Diane says, as she goes to attend to her three nieces.

Chapter Twelve

Monique and her friend Leah are chillin' in the middle of the day, in the mall's food court. Even though Monique is enjoying her friend's company, she is still stewing about the last inter-action she had with Rodney. So, she decides to vent.

"Girl…, let me tell you what happened to me the other night," Monique begins.

"Girl, what happened? Tell me," Leah responds eagerly, as she leans toward Monique, ready to hear a hot tidbit from her girlfriend.

"I was with Rodney at the movies. It was a movie I had been waiting to see, but before it could begin I started cramping. And, believe me, it was nothing nice. And, of all times, I had to run out of supplies while I was with him. I asked that fool to take me to the store on our way back to my place, and he got an attitude because me and 'my situation' caused a shift in his little plans. You know what I mean?"

"Wow, girl! I know what you mean. That sucks that he doesn't understand. That's just not right!" Leah says as she looks across the food court, spotting her friend Vanessa walking with another woman. "Oh, hold up. I see someone I know. Let me holla at her for a second," Leah says as she rises from the table.

Monique takes the interruption all in stride. "I'm straight," she says as she waves her hand, telling Leah to go.

Leah stands up from the table and heads toward Vanessa. "Hey, Nessa. What's up? What you doin'?" Then, she pauses to acknowledge Monique who is sitting there looking on. Leah points to her and says, "That's my homegirl Monique."

Vanessa answers, "Nothing, just hanging out with my friend Sharon before she goes to work." Then, as they get nearer to where Monique is sitting, introductions are made all around. "Sharon, this is Leah and Mo… Monique."

Monique, with a face lacking expression, greets the two women, "What's up."

Sitting back down, Leah invites Vanessa and Sharon to sit with them. "Y'all want to chill? We're just sitting here having girl talk." Vanessa looks at Sharon to see what she wants to do. Sharon shrugs her shoulders, and they each grab a chair, joining Monique and Leah at the table.

Monique, still with an attitude, says, "Sometimes, I can't stand men! I swear, sometimes I feel they only have one thing on their mind twenty-four seven."

Sharon chimes in, "I feel you on that, my sistah! My man called me and wanted to hook up, but because I had started my cycle, he tripped out big time!"

Seeing that she and Sharon shared a common experience, Monique says, "Girl, tell me about it! My boyfriend did the exact same thing. We were at the movies, and my cycle started. He tripped out on me. He was really feeling himself!"

At a nearby table, two other women are sitting. The voices and conversation of the four women caught their attention, so the two women look over to them. Leah sees them looking, so she turns her attention to them. Again, as with Vanessa, Leah recognizes someone she knows. "Keisha, is that you?" she asks.

"Hey, girl. What's up, Leah?"

"I almost did not recognize you. Your hair is cute..." Leah remarks, admiring her friend's new look.

"Thank you," Keisha says, as she twists her head from one side to the other, taking in the compliment. Walking over to the table, she spots Vanessa another one of her friends. "What's up, Vanessa." Then, she introduces the woman she is with. "This is my friend Janelle."

Vanessa chimes in when she sees her friend Keisha. "Hey, how are you. Leah's right... your hair is very pretty. It fits your face."

Keeping her attention trained on Keisha, Leah asks, "What's up! So, what y'all doin'?"

"Nothing. Just over here talking about her boyfriend Rodney who is trippin' on her once again," Vanessa answers while shaking her head in pity. Both Monique's and Sharon's heads turn at the same time when Rodney's name is mentioned.

"Rodney? What a coincidence! We both have

boyfriends named Rodney," Monique says to Janelle, who has been sitting there quietly.

Sharon can't hold back. She decides to jump in the conversation. "Wait! Hold up! My man's name is Rodney, too!" Monique and Sharon begin to wonder if by chance they could be speaking about the same man.

Monique doesn't waste any time trying to get to the bottom of what seems to be a weird coincidence that she and Sharon both had a situation about their cycles with their boyfriend who happens to be named Rodney. And, Janelle just so happens to have a boyfriend trippin' out her on with the same name. "Hold the hell up! I know we are not talking about the same man. Janelle, Sharon, where does this Rodney live?" Monique asks, standing to her feet.

Janelle is frantic and cannot believe her day has taken such a drastic turn from sitting at the table with Keisha to being in a group of six women discussing issues with boyfriends. Answering Monique's question, Janelle says, "1354 W. Fifth Street," hoping her boyfriend's address does not match up with either one of theirs.

Before anyone else can respond, Sharon agrees, "Yep! 1354 W. Fifth Street." Everybody goes wild and begins talking at once. Monique confirms that her boyfriend Rodney lives at the same address. The three women look at each other sizing the others up. Their friends Vanessa, Leah, and Keisha are blown away by the tailspin, too.

Keisha yells, "This ain't even right!"

Leah screams, "OMG!"

Then, Vanessa comes up with a plan. "If I were y'all, I

would go over there…" Taking in Vanessa's suggestion, the voices rise again, and no one can hear anyone else because all the women are trying to talk at one time. As the seconds tick away, the arguing and commenting becomes very heated. People who are in the nearby vicinity cannot enjoy their meals due to the commotion.

Finally, Monique tries to calm everyone down. "Wait, wait, wait…" she says, gaining their attention. "I have an idea. Why don't we set a trap for his behind?"

Janelle interrupts, "Now, I know why he asked me if I was cramping or anything. He struck out with y'all and was trying to get busy with me! That bastard!"

Regaining their attention, Monique asks, "Ladies, what do you think? Can we work together on this?" Sharon and Janelle look at Monique and at each other and nod their heads in agreement.

Chapter Thirteen

In a beautiful five-star restaurant, Valerie and Gordon are sitting at a table in the middle of the restaurant having lunch. As they enjoy good food, each other's company, and a chilled glass of semi-sweet red wine, Valerie swallows a tasty morsel of filet mignon and says, "Thanks for inviting me to lunch. The food here is delicious."

"Oh, the pleasure is all mine," Gordon says, all smiles. Looking at her with love in his eyes, Gordon raises his glass. Valerie, with love and admiration in her eyes, follows Gordon's lead and lifts her glass as well. "To the most beautiful, intelligent, extraordinary woman who has graced me with her presence from the moment I met her."

"Thank you, honey. That's sweet," she says blushing, as she takes a sip from her glass.

At a nearby table, over in a corner, a couple is sitting very close together, with their arms wrapped around each other. The man leans in and kisses the woman tenderly on the lips. Their movement catches Gordon's attention, and he peers in their direction, recognizing the woman. "Well, I'll be damned!" he says, half under his breath. Valerie turns her head to see what has caused his change in mood. When she sees the couple, she completely forgets about his reaction, as she has one of her own.

"I can't believe this. Do you see that couple over there in the corner booth all hugged up?"

"Do I? Yeah, that's my ex-girlfriend. That is the not-so-virtuous woman that I was telling you about. I guess ole boy is the one she was cheating with."

Valerie cannot contain her emotions. "You're kidding me! I have to get out of here!" Suddenly, she rises from her chair, snatches her jacket and handbag from the back of it, and heads toward the door.

"Wait! Where are you going?" Gordon's words reach dead air because Valerie is already several yards away. Gordon catches up to her outside the front door. "Valerie, wait!" he says as he reaches her. "What's wrong? Why did you leave like that?" He is thoroughly confused by her actions. *Was she upset because I got upset when I saw my ex?* he wonders. He reaches for her arm, but she shrinks back from his touch.

"Let me go!" she says with force.

"Valerie, talk to me. What is going on?" Gordon pleads.

"You don't understand. The guy at the booth… That fool is my ex! And, to top it off, he is with your ex."

"Say what! Wait a minute! You mean to tell me.... that man in there is your ex? What type of sick game is this? You can drop the surprise act! You probably knew all along that they were together! Wait! Did you get with me to get back at them? Here, it is all this time, I thought you were different from all the other ladies.... but, I guess not! You females are so vindictive! Y'all would go to the ends of the earth to get revenge! I can't believe this!"

Valerie is standing there with her mouth open, wondering how Gordon could even form his mouth to say the words that were coming from it. She is abundantly appalled, and she wastes no time letting him know. "Oh, hell no! You're thinking too highly of yourself! When we first met, you came up to my table. Do you remember that? So, how could I have planned to get with you for revenge? If I was trying to get with you, I would have approached you, don't ya think?" She did not give him a moment to respond. She kept letting her words fly. "Let me share something with you. I admit that I had seen you from time to time at church, and that was it until I saw you at the coffee shop. I didn't know you then, and now that you're accusing me of something like this, I wish I didn't know you now! I can't believe that you think that I would stoop so low to do some dumb stuff like that! How dare you! I thought better of you, Gordon! But, I see where your mind is." Valerie is so upset, tears are streaming from her eyes.

Gordon is equally as angry and dumbfounded by the turn of events; he cannot even process what Valerie is saying. He looks at her with an evil stare and says, "Didn't you say you need to go?" Her words have not computed in his mind. He just wants her out of his sight because he believes she is up to no good.

Feeling dismissed and not believing he had not taken in a word she had said, she turns to leave. "I hate you, Gordon

Benson. I'm sorry I even shared my table with you that day. Lose my number, my email, my everything! I never want to see you again!" She storms over to the valet parking attendant and hands him her ticket. The tears keep flowing down her face. She is hurt because she had finally let her walls down, thinking she could trust him with her heart.

Gordon re-enters the restaurant and sits at the table. He thinks about finishing his food, but he can't stomach it. The couple is still there, acting lovey dovey, and their presence sickens him. Gordon pays the bill and leaves, with his heart in his hands. He doesn't know what to do or where to turn. He heads to the pier to take a ride on his yacht.

Chapter Fourteen

On the other side of town, Diane is at a car dealership, hoping to purchase another car. Sitting at a desk in the manager's office, she is waiting with anticipation. The manager is trying to get her approved or at least pre-qualified, but his computer is running a tad slowly. Not wanting to discourage her with all the waiting, he makes a suggestion, "Why don't you take a walk through our lot of fine vehicles. See if there is one or two that catch your eye."

Taking his suggestion, Diane walks out to the lot and begins to browse around. An eager salesman spots her and heads in her direction. She sees him approaching, but ignores his presence. He is hoping to make eye contact with her, to get a sense of her mood and her level of seriousness regarding her car venture. "Hello there," he calls to Diane as he gets nearer. She looks up and gives a brief nod, but fails to respond. "How's your day going?" he continues professionally.

Diane relents and says, "It could be better…"

The salesman's eyebrows lift, but he doesn't know what to say, so he simply introduces himself with his hand extended. "I'm George."

Diane completely ignores his hand and continues to look at the royal blue Nissan Sentra she is standing next to, peering through the windows. "I like this one," she says. "Can you get the key, so I can start it up? I would like to hear how the engine sounds."

George, staying positive, responds, "Sure. No problem. I will be right back." After retrieving the key from the office, George removes the security lockbox and hands Diane the key. She sits inside, places the key in the ignition, turns, and nothing happens. She turns her head toward George and lifts her eyebrows, without saying a word. She turns the key again. Still- nothing. George, with an embarrassed look on his face says, "Uhhh, sometimes maintenance doesn't close the door all the way after cleaning the cars. Let me go get a battery charger."

"A battery charger? Oh, wow! My goodness. Um hum," Diane says. Ignoring her comment, George heads to the maintenance area to retrieve a battery charger. He returns with a maintenance man, who promptly attempts to charge the car's battery. With the charger attached to the proper cables, George tries to start the car, but it won't even turn over.

"This is strange," George says, thoroughly embarrassed at the entire situation. "I am so sorry about this."

Diane becomes impatient with the entire situation. "How are you guys selling cars that don't work?" George opens his mouth to defend the dealership, but another voice is heard over the loud speaker summoning him to the office. He nods at Diane, signaling to her that he needs to see what is going on inside. "Give me a minute. I'll be right back."

In the office, the manager says, "It doesn't look to good for that lady."

"Why not? A repo?" George asks.

"Try eight!" the manager responds. "Her credit history is twenty pages long! For us to give her a car, she would need to put down at least three or four grand!" George's eyes got big.

"I'll let her know," George said, as he walked back outside to Diane. When he reached Diane, he didn't mention the money. He decided to try a different tactic. "My boss said you may want to bring up your credit score before purchasing a vehicle."

"That's because of the repos I have. But, I know plenty of people who have repos and where able to buy cars."

"Yes, you can get a car with one repo or maybe two, but you have eight," George said matter-of-factly to Diane, not sparing her feelings.

"Eight? Yeah, right. I will admit to six. Maybe seven... but, eight? No, I don't care what Experian, Equifax..."

"Trans Union," George cut in with an attitude.

"Whoever! I don't care what the credit bureaus have to say about it. They are not always right. Look, I have $500 right now to put down. What can I get, Barney?"

"My name is George."

"Whatever! What can I get?"

"Hold on. Let me see what I can do." George gives Diane a fake smile and walks away, knowing his efforts will be hope-less.

"Now, that's what I'm talking about! You do that…, idiot!" As George goes back inside the office, Diane takes out her cellphone and calls the office for the second time that day. When Mr. Thomas gets on the phone, Diane tells him, "I'm in the area."

"Really!" he yells. "Diane, you said you would be late. It is 2:45!"

"And??" she asks, playing dumb.

"Your shift ends at 3:00!"

"Oh, well. I guess I will see you tomorrow then," Diane informs her boss. He gives her a brief lecture about missing work and reminds her there is much to be done.

Diane ends the call with Mr. Thomas just as George is walking back over to her. He tells her there is actually something they can do for her, but she has to fill out the paperwork. Diane, feeling good about her new vehicle, follows George to the office. After about thirty minutes, Diane is ready to roll! She gets into her vehicle, pulls to the edge of the driveway, waits for cars to pass by, then she pulls out in her shiny new golf cart!

Chapter Fifteen

After the restaurant fiasco with Gordon, it took virtually no time at all for Valerie's barriers to return. She closed herself off emotionally after her ex-boyfriend had dumped her for the woman he was 'flinging' with. After meeting Gordon, the walls slowly slipped down. Now, they are fully engaged again. Despite her emotional trauma, Valerie still believes in full devotion to God. He is the only one she knows won't hurt her. So, on an early Wednesday evening, she heads to church for weekly Bible Study.

Walking into the church, Valerie greets those she sees standing around before she reaches the group of ushers who are eager to serve. Raul, the head usher, escorts her to a seat. With a slight smile of gratitude, Valerie says, "Thank you," as she sits down on a comfortable pew.

Not much later, Gordon arrives to the church anticipating a great, spirit-filled message. When Gordon is in any church service, whether it is a Sunday morning worship service or Bible Study, a spirit of humility overshadows him. After Gordon steps into the foyer, Kent, an usher shows him to a seat. Gordon's mood is melancholy. With a nondescript face, he says, "Thanks," to Kent, who quickly shakes

Gordon's hand.

Beginning the service on time, doing all things decently and in order, the preacher approaches the podium, gaining every-one's attention. After he greets everyone, he says, "Before we get started, everyone take a moment to go around and hug at least three people." Everyone, including Valerie, immediately scans the crowd to see which three people she will approach for a quick embrace. In her inconspicuous scan, she notices Gordon. And, as expected, she avoids him at all cost. After the quick hug fest, everyone returns to their seats. Then, the preacher gives a sermonette on forgiveness. How appropriate!

As soon as Bible Study ends, Valerie wastes no time heading out to her car. Gordon had already planned to attempt to speak with her. Catching up to her in the parking lot, he reaches for her arm. "Valerie, can I talk with you for a minute?"

Pulling her arm back, Valerie says, "There's nothing to say!" Her tone and demeanor are adamant.

"Valerie, please! I'm sorry for the way I acted. I didn't mean to take my frustration out on you when I saw my ex-girlfriend. I was an ass; I realize that. I'll never do that again! I'm so sorry to have hurt you. Valerie, I need you. Please, please forgive me!"

Valerie looks surprised at the candor of his words. But, the hurt she is experiencing runs deep. She says, "The words you said to me that day cut deep." She pauses to catch her breath. "No, no! I can't do this. Leave me alone! I don't have anything to say. I will never give you the chance to hurt me again!" She wants to continue walking to her car, but Gordon has positioned his body in a way that prevents her from moving forward. So, she stands there shaking her head.

Continuing to plead his case, Gordon says, "If you can forgive me this one time, I swear I'll be the best man to you for the rest of your life. If I knew how to sing, I would sing, 'I'm sorry.'" Then, with a made-up mind, he says, "Forget it!" and goes for it. He goes all out and begins to sing, knowing his voice is bound to crack and strain. Serenading her, Gordon sings, "Valerie, I'm sorry. I will go to the end of the earth to show ya. Valerie, I'm so sorry. I didn't mean to hurt you. I love you, Valerie."

Gordon's attempt to salvage their relationship with his corny antics makes Valerie smile although she is still fuming. He is actually beginning to impress her- again. But, is it enough? Noticing her smile, Gordon stops singing. Valerie looks at him intently and inquires, "What am I going to do with you? You hurt me!"

Gordon, not knowing what else to say, continues with his apology, "I'm sorry! I'm so sorry! I'll never do that again. I love you. Please forgive me."

Valerie takes a deep breath and says, "I forgive you, but I have to go. Bye, Gordon!" She quickly moves around him and continues towards her car. Watching her get inside and hearing the engine start, he knows he has messed up big time.

Chapter Sixteen

Rodney is relaxing at his home and a few of his friends are over there hanging out and shooting the breeze. While they are having a blast, Rodney is frustrated. In the midst of the guys joking around and goofing off, they notice Rodney is not behaving as his normal loud, talkative, and arrogant self.

Joe asks Rodney, "Man, why you so stressed? You pacing back and forth and carrying on. What you going through?"

Michael doesn't give Rodney a chance to answer before supplying his own theory, "It's probably those females he's messing with." Everyone breaks out into laughter. Everyone except Rodney.

Finally taking note of Rodney's stress level, Robert yells over, "Man, chill out! Get a drink and watch the game!"

Ignoring all of their comments, Rodney provides an explanation for his sour mood, "These women and their cycles, man! It's crazy! I tried to set up a little somethin' with each of them- you know what I mean! Tell me this- why did they all have to start at the same time? I thought I had their schedules pegged!" He chuckles, mostly at himself, knowing he is off his game. "I must be slipping!" he says to himself.

Mike says, in an attempt to shift the atmosphere from half-gloom/half-lighthearted to one of complete light heartedness, "I got somethin' that will settle all this! All you have to do is get with someone else and handle your business! There! Case solved! Next topic, can we get some food up in this piece?" All four of the guys laugh, and the atmosphere shifts.

"Man, you crazy! I'm not trying to get with no one else. I'm straight with my three main ingredients." Rodney laughs along with his boys, but on the inside, he feels bad about how he treated his women.

Robert jumps in with a quick-witted response. "Okay, playa playa. You know the rule: Don't get caught!"

Rodney does not hesitate with his answer, letting his true arrogant nature show. "Is that a little hateration I hear? Fool, ain't nobody going to get caught! I'm the man! I give'em what they need when they need it! Plus, I always cover my tracks. They'll never find out about each other. I got this!"

Chapter Seventeen

Monique, Janelle, and Sharon are sitting in a dimly lit bar at a table with every kind of drink imaginable spread across it. It's Wednesday night, in the middle of the week, and they figure tonight is good a time as any to devise a plan. As they sit there drinking themselves into oblivion, they scheme and plot about how they are going to exact revenge on Rodney for triple timing them. They spend a couple of hours going around and around, until they realize they are too drunk to make sense. They are doing more laughing and asking each other, "What did you say?" between sips of this drink or that drink, as their words begin to slur. Finally, they retire to their own homes for the night. They vow to get together again to come up with a solid plan.

Chapter Eighteen

Early Thursday morning, Leah, Keisha, and Vanessa are all carpooling over to Diane's house to pick her up for work. When Vanessa pulls up, she doesn't see Diane waiting outside, so she drives to Diane's garage, blows her horn, and yells from the car window, "Diane! What you doing, girl? Let's go to work, so we can make that dolla!" Diane doesn't answer right away, and the ladies look at each other, wondering where she is.

A few minutes later, Diane walks out the front door, with a look of non-concern written all over her face. Again, they look at each other wondering what is going on. Leah asks, "Girl, are you ready?"

"I'm not riding with y'all today. I have transportation now. I tried calling you, Vanessa, to let you know, but you didn't answer your phone."

Leah is really anxious to know what is going on. "You bought a car? Oh, we have to see this. What kind of car did you buy? With your credit, I know you probably got a Jag, a Mercedes, or a Cadillac! Open that garage, girl! Let us see what you are working with!" All the ladies jump out of Vanessa's car. They are excited for their friend, and they want a chance to look at her new wheels.

As Diane opens the garage door, she says, "It's none of those. I got something better. It's a gas saver!" As the door opens, they all wonder what type of car saves gas. Then, they see the golf cart. They are in shock. Once again, their heads turn towards one another, but they are speechless, completely at a loss for words. The only sound that can be heard are sharp gasps. "So, what y'all think? I know y'all like it. Different, huh? Don't it just make you want to holla?"

"Uh, pretty much. Yeah, I kinda want to holla," Vanessa said with her eyes glued to the vehicle.

"Ummm....ufff! I'm lost for words," Keisha finally gets out, trying to hold back her laughter.

Then, Vanessa notices a cord going from the vehicle to the wall. "Why do you have it plugged in? Is this a hybrid?" At that moment, none of them can hold back any longer. Laughter erupts from all of their bellies.

Leah, who has been standing there stunned, can't hold back any longer. "Am I the only one to see that this... is a... golf cart?! Diane... what were you thinking, girl? What are you going to do when it rains? Baby girl, there are no windows, or doors for that matter!"

"I'm so lost for words," Keisha continues to say, standing there with her hands on her hips and her head shaking from side to side.

Diane assures them, "It's going to be alright. I'm straight!" Then, preparing to head off to get her day started, she gets into her new vehicle. "I'm on my way to Mickey D's and then to the Aquarium of the Pacific."

The women look at each other and back to Diane. "Stop playing. Girl, you got jokes," Vanessa says to Diane. Then, seeing the serious look on Diane's face, Vanessa asks, "Are you serious?"

"Yep, 100%. I have never been to the Aquarium before, and today, I want to do something different. I'm tired of the same ole thing."

"You did something different when you bought this," Vanessa gestures toward the golf cart. "Wasn't that enough? What about work?"

Diane looks disgusted at the mention of their job. "Been there, done that! Trust, there is nothing new about that job I want to see. So today, I am on my way to see something else."

Leah suddenly sees Diane's perspective about work. "I know that's right! You want some company?"

Diane gets excited about the prospect of having a tag-along. "I don't mind. Let's go and check out Shamoo. You can ride with me."

Leah gives the cart a once over, steps back and says to Diane, "In your golf cart! Oh, hell naw! That would be a negative! I can't be seen in that!"

Slightly offended, Diane says, "Un un! Don't hate on Poncho!"

Finally finding her words, Keisha spurts out, "Who is Poncho? I know you didn't give it a name! We can take Vanessa's car because I want to go, too. Don't you want to go too, Vanessa! We can't all fit in Poncho, so won't you drive us?" Keisha gives Vanessa the puppy dog eyes look.

Vanessa begins to cough. "Oh, I'm not feeling well today. We need to call in."

Chapter Nineteen

Early Friday morning, Valerie wakes up ready for another uneventful day at the office. She has some files to close, and she expects it to be a mellow, low-key day because at least two people are taking vacation and her boss is away at a conference. She packs her lunch, leftovers from the night before, not wanting to leave the building during lunch-hour traffic.

In the midst of the flow Valerie has created for her day, she picks up the phone to call a client. Just as the client answers the phone, she hears a light tap on her office door. Asking the client to hold on, she says, "Come in." Waiting to see who is interrupting her flow, Valerie tilts her head towards the door, so she can see who will walk in. Someone answers, but all Valerie can see are the legs of the person. Covering the person's face and most of the upper body is a tall and wide crystal vase filled with four dozen long-stemmed red roses.

Valerie immediately place of the caller on an extended hold by pushing the mute button and rises from her desk. Her mouth is in the shape of an "O." Reading the surprise on her face, the deliverer smiles brightly. He loves seeing the look of excitement on the receivers' faces. Valerie thanks the deliverer as she leans over and takes in the sweet aroma.

After Valerie completes the call, her head is still spinning from the gift that causes a special radiance in her office. She finds it hard to concentrate on work, so she decides to leave her office for a bit of fresh air. In her car, she can't decide on a destination, so she drives home. At least there, she will have peace and quiet. Unlocking the front door, Val walks in with a single rose she had taken from the vase. She wanted to keep a bit of the ambience with her. Immediately making herself comfortable, she kicks off her pumps and slides onto the sofa. She allows her body to a moment to relax, as her head rests on a throw pillow.

Just as she begins to doze off, the sound of the doorbell interrupts her nap. Lifting her head, Valerie wonders who knows she is at home. Valerie opens the front door and immediately steps back, shocked by what she sees. Actually, all she can see is a cloud of red balloons. Then, a young lady moves her head around the balloons and smiles at Valerie. "It must be your lucky day," she says, as she hands Valerie a large box of assorted chocolates and the cloud of red balloons – four dozen balloons to be exact.

"Wow," Valerie says in amazement, as she receives her second gift of the day. "Thank you," she says, as her heart leaps.

Valerie decides to tie the balloons all over the living room and in her bedroom. But, her head is growing foggier her by the moment. She knows Gordon has sent the gifts and is trying to get her back. As much as she wants to run into his arms and get back together with him, she doesn't want to be vulnerable and open herself to more heartache. Logically though, she knows she can't avoid pain for her entire life. That's no way for anyone to live.

Valerie decides she can't think with the single rose and all the balloons staring her in the face, not to mention the box of chocolates. She grabs her handbag and keys and heads out to her car. Not ready to return to work, she heads to Marina Del Rey.

Leaning against the railing on the pier, she notices a boat passing by with an inscribed name just like all the other boats. This one in particular catches her attention because the name reads "My Valerie." Valerie's breath catches in her throat, and a single tear springs from her eye. Lost in thought, Valerie doesn't notice the boat pulling close to the pier. She only takes notice when Gordon is standing on the boat deck two yards away from her.

Snapping out of her trance, she sees him and says, "Hello?" as if though she can't believe it's really him. First, the flowers at the office. Then, the balloons and candy at home. Now, he's here at the marina? She tries hard to take it all in.

"Valerie, please forgive me," Gordon requests.

"I told you at church that I forgave you. By the way, thank you for all the roses and candy."

"You are welcome, sweetheart. It is my pleasure. Will you do me a huge favor?"

Having no idea what he is about to ask her, Valerie

answers, "Maybe."

"Will you come around to the boat port?"

Guessing his request is harmless, Valerie consents. "Okay, give me a few minutes."

In Gordon's mind, he is not going to take any more chances of losing Valerie again. He figures this is his moment, and he is going all out. Once Valerie comes around to meet him at the boat port, Gordon takes her hand and assists her with climbing aboard the yacht. Once she is safe and secure, he speaks lovingly to her. "Valerie, hear me out on this. When I saw my ex-girlfriend, the wound was re-opened all over again, but instead of me thinking it through, I reacted prematurely. And, when you told me the man she was with was your ex-boyfriend, I couldn't take it. But even through it all, I still do not want her back. Valerie, it's you I want. When I saw you cry that day, I knew I was wrong, and I am so sorry for that. Believe me, I love you very much." Without waiting for Valerie to respond, Gordon reaches for a red velvet box and gets down on one knee. "Valerie, will you marry me?"

Valerie doesn't know what to make of it all. In a state of shock, she stutters as she responds to his marriage proposal. "Gordon, I… I… love you, too. Yes! Yes! I'll marry you!" Gordon stands up, places both arms around her waist, and gives her a passionate kiss, while lifting her off the floor. Their kiss lingers on for quite a while. When they come up for air, both of them have tears running down their faces.

Releasing his embrace, Gordon reaches into his back

pocket and takes out his wallet. "Now, I know weddings are all about the bride and her dress, so here, take this credit card. You shouldn't have any problems with it; the skies the limit. All I ask is for you to let me know when and where to show up. The entire wedding details and planning are in your hands."

Still in a state of disbelief, Valerie takes the credit card, looks at it and back up to Gordon. "Gordon, do you know what you're doing?"

With love in his eyes, Gordon looks at her and says, "I know you're going to call some of your girlfriends and plan our beautiful day for us. And, I also know this – I'm not taking any more chances of letting you out of my life. I love you that much." Valerie responds to his words with a passionate kiss.

Chapter Twenty

Rodney had not contacted any of his women after the blow up he had with each of them. Nevertheless, the women decide it is time to put their plan into action. At their last planning session, Monique was selected to get the ball rolling. So, she gives Rodney a call. He is at the fish market when the call comes in. At first, he doesn't know if he should answer or not. Finally, on the last ring, he decides to answer. When Monique hears his voice, she puts the plan in motion. Very sweetly, Monique says, "Hi, Rodney."

Rodney responds, "Monique?" Not certain if it's her voice he is hearing.

"Uh, yeah… It's me. Were you expecting someone else?"

"Oh no, baby. I don't have anybody else. It's just you all the way. Listen… I'm sorry about how I acted towards you earlier this week. I was completely out of line. Do you forgive me?"

Monique has a calm attitude about the whole thing. "Don't sweat it, Rod. I ain't trippin!"

Rodney cannot believe his ears and his luck. He was sure she was going to read him the riot act. Seeing how calm she is, he decides to test his luck. "So, what's up, baby?" he asks, trying to get a feeling about whether she wants to see him. Surprising him even further, Monique takes full responsibility for their misunderstanding.

"I know I kinda messed things up. So, I want to make it up to you." Rodney cannot believe his ears, but he doesn't say anything. "Do you have any plans for tonight?" she asks.

Eager to move the conversation forward, Rodney answers, "No, I'm off work. What do you have in mind?"

"I'll put it this way, can you come over around eight?"

"Make it 7:59," Rod says with much swag, beginning to feel like his old self. After Rod and Monique disconnect the call, Rodney's confidence is rapidly coming back. Things went so well with Monique, he thinks he should give it a try with Sharon. Still waiting for his order at the fish stand, he dials Sharon's number. When she answers, he goes straight in for the score, using a familiar greeting. "Sharon, baby how are you doing?"

Unlike Monique, Sharon doesn't have a sweet demeanor. She displays a pissed-off attitude. "Baby!" she yells. "Don't 'baby' me! What do you want, Rodney?"

"I'm calling to say I'm sorry. I would like to make up for how I acted. I wasn't sensitive to what you were going through, and I know it wasn't right. You know I love you, right?"

"Love me? What? You don't love me!" Sharon yells, continuing to give Rodney the blues.

"Baby, don't say that. I do love you, and to show it, I want to make it up to you in a couple of days."

Fully understanding that Monique must have made her call and set up plans to see Rodney, Sharon knows why he has to wait two days. But, she acts oblivious and asks, "Why in a couple days?" She waits for the lie that will most certainly come next.

"Awhh... because I have some business that I have to take care of. One of my boys caught a case, and I have to go help him out."

"One of your friends? I don't know why you even hang around them. The only thing they ever do is get into trouble."

Basically ignoring her retort, Rodney continues with trying to set up their date. "So, I will see you in a couple of days, okay?"

"Are you sure? Don't be lying to me!" Sharon yells, continuing to play the role.

"Yeah, I'm positive. Besides, I have some making up to do. I've been away from you way too long. Sharon, I want you to think about this, and don't say nothing. I want to tell you... I love you, girl. Don't say nothing. Later." Rodney disconnects the call, leaving something on Sharon's mind. But, she doesn't fall for it. Not for one moment.

After Rodney sweet-talks Sharon, his number is called to pick up his fish order. As he drives away, he says to himself, "One more to go." He is feeling good. After taking a couple bites of red snapper, he picks up his phone and dials Janelle. When she answers, he says, "Hi, baby. It's me, Rodney. Don't say anything; just hear me out on this. I'm sorry for what I did to you and how I treated you earlier this week. I want to make it up to you if you will let me."

Janelle is out shopping, and she has already made up in her mind about her and Rodney's relationship and is ready to play her part in the plan she made with Monique and Sharon. Calmly, she says, "There is nothing to make up for. It's over between us. So, you don't ever have to call me anymore." She continues to browse through the dress section, looking for a nice evening dress. Rodney is alarmed. Her words come to him unexpectedly.

To appease her, he says, "Janelle baby, we have history together, and I'm not trying to let you go. I love you! You should know this by now!"

Not receiving Rodney's words, she responds, "What I know is that you hung up in my face, and now you're calling me talking about you love me! I don't think so! That is not my definition of love. Understand this, love doesn't live here anymore!"

Feeling as though Janelle is truly done with him, Rodney pleads his case. "Please, Janelle! Give me one more chance, and if I mess up again, you can leave me. Please, let me make it up to you. Three days, just give me three days, and I'll be over to see you."

Immediately, Janelle replies, "I don't even know why am asking… but why three days?"

"Because one of my homeboys caught a case, and I have to go out of town to help him."

"I'm only going to give you three days, and if you mess up one more time, you are going to find yourself missing! I shouldn't even give you another chance!"

"I got you. In three days, it's going to be just you and me

baby all the way. As a matter fact, while I'm gone, think about moving in with me. Don't say anything right now. We'll talk about it when I see you. Do you still love me?"

"You know I love you, boo. You be careful, okay? I'll see you in three days. Bye, baby." Everything Janelle said was just part of the plan that she concocted with Sharon and Monique. Although she convinced Rodney she is on board, she didn't fall for any of his wasted lines.

Meanwhile, Rodney has made it home and is sitting at the dining room table. He places his food on the table and congratulates himself. "Yeah! That's what I'm talking about... Who's the man? I'm the MAN!"

Chapter Twenty- One

The ladies are at the Aquarium of the Pacific, joking around and having loads of fun. As they walk through the aquarium, they gaze at the different sights as they laugh and talk with one another. They walk past the shark lagoon, gazing at the different variations of shark, and finally, they end up at the Animal Encounter. Leah decides she wants to feed the seals, but the other ladies aren't interested. So, they sit back and watch Leah enjoying herself.

When lunchtime approaches, they decide to take a break for lunch at the food court. While they are eating, Mr. Thomas, back at the office, looks around and gets a strange feeling. Many of his workers are out that day. His secretary had told him each time someone called in, but he had not realized how many there actually were out until he saw all of the empty desks. He decides to give each one a call and find out what is really going on.

Just as they place their food on the table, Keisha stands up and says, "I'll be right back. I need to go to the ladies' room."

"I'll go with you because I need to go, too," Leah says.

As Keisha and Leah walk away from the lunch table,

Vanessa's phone rings. "Helloooo?" she answers.

On the other end, Mr. Thomas is taking in the sound of her voice. "Vanessa?" he greets her.

Surprised to hear her boss' voice, Vanessa pulls the phone away from her ear and looks at her caller ID. Sounding sick, she asks, "God?"

"God! No, it's Mr. Thomas. You don't sound too well. Don't try to go outside today. Get some rest. Hope to see you soon."

Vanessa, still putting on her sick act, replies, "Okay. Bye, Moses!"

Inside the bathroom, Keisha is washing her hands as her phone begins to ring. Completely catching her off guard, she doesn't bother to look at the caller ID. "Hello?"

Mr. Thomas says, "Keisha, this is Mr. Thomas. I'm calling to see if you're okay."

Keisha becomes nervous and tries to think fast on her feet. "My head is burning up. I'm splashing water on it now, so I can cool down… Oooh!"

"I am so sorry to hear that. I hope you feel better soon. Get some rest."

Next, Diane's cell phone rings, then rings, and rings again. But, she does not answer it. Vanessa looks at her and says, "Girl, it is Mr. Thomas calling you. You'd better answer!"

Diane rolls her eyes at Vanessa and says, "He doesn't pay me enough to talk to him when I'm sick." Keisha and Leah have made it back to the table at that point. They all burst into laughter.

The ladies take their time eating their lunch as they continue to laugh and joke around and talk about how sick they supposedly are. Once they're done eating, Keisha says, "Now, let's go finish sightseeing and enjoy our sick day."

Chapter Twenty-Two

On Friday afternoon, Valerie is sitting at her dining room table with a host of bridal magazines and her laptop, looking through each one, along with a host of websites to find the perfect wedding dress. Her excitement is almost over-whelming. She can't seem to contain herself, and she is growing more and more anxious by the moment. As she scans through one of the websites, she sees a dress that catches her eye. "This is cute, but that's way too much," she says, looking at the four-digit price. Reminding herself of Gordon's words, she gets excited. "Oh now, wait a minute... Gordon did say the sky's the limit. But, I'm going to need some help with all this wedding stuff. Let me call my cousin Diane. She may be good with all of this."

Diane is driving along on her new golf cart when her phone rings. She presses her foot on the brake and reaches down to grab her purse to get her phone out. "Hello?"

"Hi, cousin."

"Who's this?"

"It's me Valerie."

"What's going on, girl? I haven't heard from you in a while."

"I need your help."

"What do you need? I'll help you out. Just don't ask me for any money 'cause I'm broke."

"No, Di, it's not about money. I'm getting married. I wanted to see if you will be my maid of honor. And guess what?" Valerie does not wait for Diane to consent to being her maid of honor because she already knows Diane is open to being on display for a crowd at any time. Valerie is more interested in sharing her good news with her.

"What?" Diane asks.

"My fiancé gave me a credit card and told me the sky is the limit!" All of a sudden, the other line of the phone gets quiet. "Hello? Hello, Diane?" As Valerie is waiting for Diane to respond, she hears a horn blowing outside her front window. When Valerie opens the front door, Diane is standing there. Valerie looks at her cousin suspiciously as she goes ahead and hangs up her phone. "Diane? Why did you hang up? Girl, you got here fast... Well, come on in."

"No! You come out. Let's go!"

Valerie has no idea what is on Diane's mind. With her eyebrows lifted, she asks, "Where are we going?" Then, out of the corner of her eye, she sees something sitting on her lawn. Turning her head, she asks, "What is that on my grass?"

With joy in her voice, Diane answers, "That's my new ride."

"I know we're not going in that, and that's for sure!"

"Don't hate! But, we can take your car."

Valerie and Diane walk into Valerie's house through the front door and go to the garage. After Valerie and Diane get into the car, Valerie opens the garage door and backs her car out onto the driveway. Then, she stops and looks at her cousin. Diane wonders what the issue is, so she asks, "What?"

"Oh, you can get that thing off my grass. Go ahead and park it in my garage until we come back." Diane huffs, but she does with her cousin requests.

At the bridal shop, Valerie and Diane look through many, many dresses until Valerie finds one she really likes. She puts it on and models it for Diane, who is sitting comfortably in a chair. The dress is Cinderella style, and both women find it adorable. All Diane can think about is dollar signs. She tells Valerie, "You need a dress with a long, long train."

"I do, huh?" Valerie responds.

Instead of answering Valerie's question, a thought comes to Diane's mind. "OMG! I have to call to rent and buy some things... I'm going to need that credit card."

Valerie is caught up with looking at other dresses to try on that she's not really paying too much attention to what Diane is saying. "It's in my purse. It's the gold AMX platinum."

Diane grabs Valerie's purse and begins to rifle through it. Then, she immediately picks up her phone and dials a number. "Yes, I would like to order. Wait, hold on… How many people are you looking to have, Val?"

Still eyeing herself in the full-length mirror, Valerie answers, "Maybe around fifty to seventy-five people. I don't really want a big wedding. A small to medium wedding should do just fine." She turns to head back to the dressing room with an assistant trailing behind her with two other dresses. "I'll be back in a moment with another dress on."

Returning to her phone call, Diane says, "Make it for 200. It always starts off small but ends up larger than large." She ends the call but immediately makes another one. During that phone call, she makes another order and tells the salesperson, "Yes, just charge it to the credit card. What color? Make it black. Okay. Thank you very much."

Valerie returns to the open showroom, modeling a beautiful dress with a very long train. Admiring herself in the mirror, she says, "This is sooooo beautiful!"

As Diane looks on, she has to agree. "You do look beautiful. That dress is stunning! What's his name is going to love you in that."

Valerie looks over at Diane and shakes her head. "Gordon."

Oblivious, Diane asks, "Who's Gordon?"

Placing one hand on her hip, Valerie says with a little attitude, "What's his name. I mean… my fiancé. Gordon is my fiancé."

Chapter Twenty-Three

Gordon is in an excellent mood because he is at the tuxedo shop with his seven groomsmen. Some are his brothers, and others are his close friends. They are trying on different styles of tuxedos. There is a lot of joking and teasing going on as they clown one another as they sport the various styles. Breaking their moment of fun, Gordon's third grooms-man Brian asks a serious question, "So Gordon, what made you decide to get married? I remember you saying after your last break up that you were leaving women alone for a while. Then, all of a sudden, you're talking about taking the plunge. I don't get it."

Chiming in, Jerome, one of Gordon's brothers, says, "Yeah, man. You were talking about how women are trifling! What makes this one any different?" Laughter erupts from the men's bellies. But, they all want to know the answer.

"I know I said all of those things, but Valerie… she is different. You know you can find women all day long who just want you to come out the pocket. Not her, she can hold her own. I like a strong independent woman."

Jerome responds, "I know that's right! Now that's the kind of woman I would like, too."

Gordon continues pumping up his woman. "We went to a basketball game, for which she has season tickets… And, I'm not talking about just for a seat. I'm talking about a private room!" That bit of information sends his boys over the edge. They are all smiles, trying to talk at the same time.

Nick says, "Yeah, you don't find too many of those running around! She sounds like she's the one. So, tell us, does she have any sisters?" All his friends and brothers who are single get a good chuckle out of that question.

"Oh, and because she's not going to make all the games, she said I can take my boys with me to those games!" Gordon continues, completely ignoring the question about Valerie having sisters. A howl can be heard from the group of men as they take in the information about the private room at the Staples Center.

Matthew jumps in. "Now, that's what I'm talking about! We love her already. What took you so long to put the ring on her finger?"

Looking a little sad, Gordon says, "Well at first, I almost lost her."

"What do you mean you almost lost her?" another one of his brothers asks.

"It was crazy, John," Gordon says looking at his brother and all the other guys. "We were having lunch and saw our exes at a booth hugged up!" The men go crazy at that point. Everyone is talking at once, trying to figure out what the heck is going on.

Nick says, "That sounds like a Jerry Springer show. Wait… was she trying to get even or something?"

"That's what I thought at first! But, she was just as much in shock as I was. Man, I was so mad. I did confront her about that very thing. After we broke up, I had to realize that she never came over to me when we first met. Actually, I went over to her, so she had no idea who I was. When all hell broke loose that day, she broke it off with me. That's not a woman who would be trying to get even. She just got caught up in the mess like I did. Now that I'm thinking about it, she was actually trying to leave before I ever found out about who the dude was."

Jerome interrupts, "Yeah man, if she was trying to leave before you even knew what was going on…"

Nick agrees, "From what you've said, she got caught off guard just like you did…"

After the conversation dies down, the men continue trying on more tuxedo styles. Gordon finally decides what he wants to wear and chooses a similar style with a different color scheme for the groomsmen. Then, they move next door to a restaurant to sit, relax, and have lunch. As they are sitting at the table, Brian asks, "I want to know something, Gordon. How in the world did you get her back after all of that drama?"

"I had to sing to her!" All the men get a kick out of that because they all know Gordon cannot sing a lick.

"I'm surprised that helped you get her back at all. Well… that's good you got her back. But, if you mess up again, I'm getting her number, and you'll be coming to my wedding!" Nick retorts. All the men burst out into laughter.

Gordon even has to laugh, as he says, "Don't get hurt!"

"I'm just saying… accusing that beautiful woman like that!" Nick continues. The men continue laughing and joking around with Gordon and with one another, as they enjoy the savory meals they ordered.

Chapter Twenty-Four

Looking forward to a pleasurable night, Rodney pulls up to Monique's house and parks at the curb. Before getting out, he checks himself in the rearview mirror for one last look. "I know I look good! Let's do this!" He walks up to the door with his usual swagger and gently knocks.

Monique opens the door and gives him a look of expectation. "Hey, baby. Come in."

As Rodney walks into her home, he gives her a tight squeeze around her waist, as she places her arms around his neck. "Again, I just want to say sorry for the way I treated you. I was trippin'."

Monique gives him a sly grin and says, "Don't worry about it. This night belongs to us, so let's enjoy it to the fullest. As a matter of fact, this night belongs just to you. Just for Rodney. Have a seat."

As Rodney takes a seat on the couch, and he can smell the sweet aroma that's coming from the kitchen. "What smells so good? What are you cooking?"

Monique is still giving a sly grin, as she answers, "Oh, that's my surprise for you. I'll be right back. Let me go and check on dinner." At that moment, the doorbell rings, but

Monique continues walking into the kitchen, as she says over her shoulder, "Baby, can you get that?"

Rodney rises to his feet with a look of disappointment on his face. In a low voice, he says, "Sure. I wonder who this is when I'm trying to get busy. I hope it's not her mother!" He walks toward the front door and without looking through the peephole, he opens it. Standing in front of him is Sharon. Sharon see the look of horror that crosses Rodney's face as she says, "You look like you just saw a ghost!"

Janelle steps from behind Sharon and says, "Or two!"

Hearing the ladies' voices, Monique joins them at the front door and sees Rodney backing away from Sharon and Janelle. She says, "Step into the light, Rodney!" They all walk toward him, backing him up into the living room. Once they get him where they want him, they all stop moving and stand in a line directly in front of him.

"What the hell is this?" he shouts.

"Don't call yo daddy just yet!" Monique shouts.

Rodney screams, "Heavenly Father!"

"This bastard is playin' them, too! So… you want to play? Okay… Get the rope!" Sharon directs.

"A rope? Oh, hell na!"

"Let's tie his ass up!" they all agree.

While Janelle and Sharon push Rodney back onto a dining room chair, Monique grabs the rope that she had ready and begins to wrap it around his legs and his arms. Janelle asks, "Monique, do you have any watermelon or any type of fruit?"

Wondering what Janelle's plan is, Monique answers, "Yeah… I have some watermelon."

Janelle gets excited and says, "It's time to do some cooking! I brought some hog head cheese, chitlins, pig feet, and some octopus. Do you have any fish grease?"

Sharon yells, "Oh, Lord! She's going to kill'em!"

Janelle looks through Monique's seasoning cabinet. "No, just going to give him something he can feel! Oh, cayenne pepper!"

Sharon looks at Monique and says, "I take it she doesn't know how to cook!"

Monique answers, "That's okay! He's going to get every-thing he deserves and then some!"

Beginning to understand that the women plan to do him harm, Rodney begins to yell. "Oh, hell to the na! It ain't going down like this! Help! Help!" He begins to jerk violently and wiggle his arms and legs, trying to get loose.

Sharon looks at Monique and says, "Get some tape, so we can shut him up!"

Chapter Twenty-Five

Still on that same afternoon, Valerie and Diane continue the wedding plans as they walk around a bakery, looking at the extravagant wedding cakes that are on display. The cakes look so tasty that their mouths begin to water. Although the cakes are beautifully decorated with some of the most spectacular designs, Valerie doesn't see anything that moves her to the point of ordering it for her own wedding. So, she takes a seat at the bakery counter where all of the wedding cake photo albums are displayed, and she begins looking through to get an idea of what she wants. Meanwhile, Diane is on the telephone.

Speaking into the phone, Diane says, "Yes, we want all of that. Sky's the limit. Valerie, what colors would you like? I already picked out your theme."

"I was thinking about gold and green. What do you mean you already picked out my theme?"

"Girl, I got this! Your day is going to be so beautiful! Trust me. Have you thought about what month you are looking at?"

"Maybe a fall wedding."

"Nope! Fall is not good for me. Don't do cold!"

Valerie tries to reason with Diane by saying, "We will be inside."

"No, you're not. I told you I already picked out your theme. A summer wedding will be better for you, and since it's right around the corner, we don't have much time."

Valerie is flabbergasted by her cousin's answer. "Why the rush? We don't have to do it that soon. We can take our time and make it perfect."

Diane looks at Valerie as if though she has lost her mind. "Have you ever been married before?"

"No, but you haven't either. So what does that have to do with anything?" Valerie is trying hard to figure out where Diane is going with her thinking.

"It has everything to do with it! I've seen enough engagements, and they didn't look too good! You don't have to wait. I've seen some ladies plan their wedding for one to two years in advance. As time went by, they end up breaking up. Then, the wedding is off, and she has to try to get her money back."

Valerie starts laughing. "Have I ever told you that you are crazy?"

"Whatever! You know I'm telling the truth. Now, we will need just a few more items, and your wedding will be finished."

"Finished! What are you talking about? Diane, you can't plan a whole wedding in two hours! It takes time. I want a perfect wedding, and two hours is not going to give me that. I'm not going to have a drive through wedding. I'm not getting married at McDonald's!" Although she is quite perturbed with what Diane is suggesting, she giggles as she makes her statement because she truly believes Diane is joking.

"Don't hate on McDonald's. Ronald can give you away, and we can give happy meals for all your guests."

As they sit there, they both imagine Ronald McDonald with his yellow and red suit with his big floppy red shoes, standing next to Valerie in her wedding gown as they walk down the aisle. Right behind them are the bridesmaids with office carts, passing out happy meals to all the guests.

Thinking out loud, Diane has one finger up to her temple as she says, "Hmmm, that's an idea!"

Valerie is really about to lose it, as Diane seems to be trying to press the idea forward. "Don't play with me, Diane!"

"Who's playing? Think about it, Val. You can save a lot of money and have everything in one shot… And, all that extra money… The things we can do! Ooooh! Thank you, Jesus!"

"No! No! No! Diane, what am I going to do with you? Have you really been talking with a wedding planner because I have doubts? Got me walking down the aisle with Ronald! I truly believe that you don't know what you're doing!"

Seeing that her cousin is about to lose it, Diane's decide to be serious for a moment. "You're going to have a beautiful wedding. Trust me. I got this!"

"Lord, give me strength! I don't know what I'm in for. Father, I'm kinda scared! Please help!" Valerie says as she lifts her head upward toward heaven.

Chapter Twenty-Six

Gordon is looking forward to marrying Valerie just as much as she is looking forward to marrying him. As she takes care of her responsibilities with the wedding planning, Gordon is thinking and planning for longevity. So, he is out house hunting, searching for a house for his beautiful bride-to-be. While he is on location at one property, standing outside by the pool, he dials Valerie's number. When she answers, he greets her. "Hi, beautiful."

Hearing his voice, makes Valerie blush. "Well, hi there. How are you doing?"

"I'm doing fine. How's my love?"

"I'm better now that I'm talking to you. Where are you right now?"

"I'm out house hunting. Hey, I have a question for you."

Wondering what he is about to ask, Valerie says, "Okay."

"Do you like swimming pools?"

"I love pools. I love water."

In the background, Diane is ear hustling. "House hunting, pool... OMG... Does he have a brother?" She starts laughing. Valerie waves her hand in her cousin's direction, shushing her.

Gordon can hear a voice in the background, and he asks, "Who is that?"

"That's my cousin Diane. She's helping me with the wedding plans. She's going to be my maid of honor."

"That's nice that you have your cousin helping you out. I can't wait to meet her. She sounds great."

"Yeah, I'm sure she's looking forward to meeting you, too. Well, I just want to warn you, she's kind of crazy!"

Gordon laughs and says, "To me, everybody has a little crazy in their family. Wait until you meet my family, a few of them are a little touched also."

Valley gets a kick out of that. "Yeah, but Diane's... How do you say it? The elevator has twenty floors, and she stops... uhhh, somewhere in the middle." She continues laughing.

"Oh wow! Should I be scared? I'm playing... She can't be that bad. Besides, as long as I have you, I'm not worried about anybody else. I love you, Valerie."

"I love you, too. And, thank you for understanding. Well, let me get back. I will talk to you later." They blow air kisses and end their call.

Chapter Twenty-Seven

Back at Monique's house, in the dining room, Rodney is still trying to break loose from the ropes that have him bound to the chair. And, he is still trying to talk through the tape that covers his mouth. He is trying to plead his case, hoping they will have mercy on him. "Let me out of here! You females are crazy!" While Rodney has been sitting there, he has been thinking about his life and how he ended up in that situation. Although he can't really blame the three women for being upset, he desperately wants to get out of there and out of their grips.

Monique interrupts his rant. "This is a special occasion. We think you deserve a special dinner." Sharon steps forward and removes the tape from his mouth, ripping it straight across and showing no mercy at all. "Ouch! I don't know how y'all think I'm going to eat that mess!" He can see what they have brewing, and he can smell the scents that wreak from it.

Sharon says, "Well, mess is what you're full of, so this feast here is right up your alley."

Janelle decides she wants part of the action. Her anger is boiling over. "Get a lighter! Let's set his behind on fire!"

Rodney sees the seriousness of the situation, and he can tell these women are not playing with him. They are definitely out for revenge. Again, he tries to plead his case, but in a calmer manner. "Look, look, a brotha's sorry. Okay? I'm sorry!" he shouts.

Janelle responds angrily, "You ain't sorry! Let's sit him behind my car while I go start it!"

Monique understands that all three of them have a reason to be pissed off. But, she believes Janelle is definitely going too far. She puts her hands up in the air towards Janelle and says, "Have you ever thought about anger management?" They had agreed that Rodney should be punished, but there was a thin line that they certainly did not want to cross.

Janelle looks at Monique as if though Monique doesn't understand her pain. "I have the right to be mad! This fool was talking about me moving in with him!"

"What? He asked you to move in with him? Really! He never asked me to move in with his sorry ass!" Sharon says.

Monique chimes in, "Me neither! I'm so sick of you! Open wide!" At that point, they begin to shove the foul smelling and horrible tasting food into his mouth. Rodney gags and gags and gags and tries to spit the food out.

"Uughh! Stop! Stop! I'm sorry! I'm sorry!"

"Oh, you're not sorry yet! You're in for a long night, my fool! Feed his ass some more!" Janelle yells.

"No! My stomach! Help! Help!"

After they feed him more of the delicacy they prepared, Sharon says, "Get that tape and shut him up again! Monique, do you have any hair clippers?"

Monique ponders for a moment with her head down and her hands on her hips. "You know what? I do. My brother left them here the last time he cut his hair."

"It's time to turn it up... Yeah... This is what happens when you try to bite off more than you can chew!" says Sharon.

When Monique finally digs out the clippers and bring them back to the ladies, Sharon takes them, plugs them in, and begins to give Rodney the haircut of his life. On one side, she cut a pattern like a checkerboard, and on the other side, it is full of zigzags. He is a sight to be seen.

Feeling as though they have tortured him enough, Monique asks her co-conspirators, "So, now what are we going to do with him?"

Janelle has a brilliant idea of course, "Let's rent a boat, take it out very far, and then toss his ass into the sea with the piranhas!"

Sharon and Monique look at each other at the sound of Janelle's suggestion. Sharon looks lovingly at Janelle and says, "You know... there is help you can get for that!"

Janelle ignores Sharon's comment. "I'm just saying... We need to teach his ass a lesson he'll never forget!"

"Uhmm, uhmm, uhmm," Rodney mutters, with the tape still across his mouth. While the ladies try to devise a plan to further their scheme, Rodney is trying to get away. He scoots and scoots his chair a little at a time and then a little bit more, trying to get closer to the front door. But, his chair falls over and gets the attention of the women.

Janelle sees him and begins laughing at his feeble attempt at getting away. "Where do you think you are going, fool?" As Sharon reaches to lift him up, Janelle continues, "Leave his ass down there for a while."

Monique objects, "Oh, hell nah! He ain't staying here!"

Janelle is still amped way up. She says, "You are so lucky I didn't bring my gun! I would've made sure you would be out of commission!"

At that point, Monique is ready to get the whole thing done and over with. She says, "I have a perfect idea. We are going to teach him a lesson of all times. I guarantee that he will not treat any more women with disrespect." She begins to fill them in on her plan without allowing Rodney to overhear. They agree and become very excited.

Once the ladies gather him up and get everything they need, they drive down a dark road where the traffic is very slow at that time of night. The next morning though, everyone who drives by will see the women's handiwork. When they are done, they wave goodbye to Rodney, who is hanging from a billboard with a feminine pad on the outside of his pants and a sign hanging around his neck that reads: Respect women.

Chapter Twenty-Eight

Valerie and Diane are driving back to Valerie's house after a full day of wedding planning, looking at cakes and gowns and everything in between. A song comes on the radio, and Diane joins in. She sings, "I'm free to do what I want, with any old thang!"

Valerie interrupts Diane's singing and says, "You sound like you're happy to be singing that." She doesn't understand her cousin's perspective and why she would put herself out there like that.

In her defense, Diane explains, "You don't know what a week I had! Having cramps is the meanest thing a female has to endure." She finally feels free after her cycle has passed, and she doesn't have pains stabbing her in the uterus.

Understanding her cousin's perspective a little better, Valerie says, "I know that's right. I'm with you on that one." Valerie pulls into her driveway and remembers Diane's golf cart is in the garage, so Valerie leaves her car there.

As the women get out of the car, they grab their bags and make their way to the front door. Diane looks over at her cousin and says, "I'm going to have to stay at your house tonight. Hope you don't mind..."

Valerie instantly responds, "I don't mind. We have been out all day long with the planning and all. We both need to get off our feet."

As if though Diane has not heard her cousin's response, she continues by saying, "Please! I can't go home because my golf cart is not that visible at night, plus my lights have been turned off, which reminds me..."

Valerie looks back at Diane as they walk through the front door. "What do you mean your lights are off?"

"Hold on just a minute. I need to make a call." Diane plops down on Valerie's couch and pulls out her cell phone and dials the electric company. "Hello, this is an emergency! My lights are turned off, and I need them back on ASAP! I know I need to pay my bill, but look, if I put five dollars on it, can you at least turn on my kitchen and bathroom lights?" The person on the other line hung up on her, finding her request ridiculous.

As Diane looks at her phone in disappointment, Valerie is on the other couch directly across from her laughing and shaking her head. When Valerie finally gets control of her laughter, she asks Diane, "How much is your light bill?"

With a pitiful look on her face, Diane answers, "Only $2,575.32. That's all."

Valerie is totally flabbergasted. "That's all! Girl, you live by yourself! What's wrong? You can't see! How in the world did your bill get that high? And, why are you driving a golf cart? Let's get down to what's really going on." As she prepares for Diane's answer, she tucks her feet under herself and gets comfortable on the couch.

"That's not for one month. That's a running tab... As far as the golf cart is concerned, I was trying to buy a car, but my credit is shot!" Tears come to Diane's eyes as she tells her cousin about her troubles. She quickly wipes them away.

Looking at her cousin with pity, Valerie says, "Your credit must be shot! So, what are you going to do? You can't keep riding around in that."

Lightheartedly, Diane says, "Don't worry. I have it all under control." She brushes the subject off as though it is a non-factor.

Interrupting their girl talk is a ring from Valerie's phone. "Hello?"

"Hi sweetie. How did it go today?" Gordon asks.

Valerie gets up from the couch and walks into her kitchen. "So far so good. Question, how do you feel about a summer wedding?"

Gordon is sitting in his living room completely relaxed after the long day he had with the guys. He is eating hot wings and sweet potato fries while watching TV. "It sounds perfect to me. You are going to make a beautiful bride. My family is going to love you, especially my mother. She's been trying to marry me off for a while. I just never found that perfect woman until now."

Valerie is blushing so hard that she can barely respond. After collecting herself, she manages to say, "I don't know what to say. I can't wait to meet your family."

Gordon replies, "I can't wait to meet your family also, especially your cousin. I think we're going to get along just fine. I'll make the arrangements for both families on the yacht. We can take a small cruise, so we can all bond. How does that sound?"

As she leans against the kitchen counter, in a dreamy voice, Valerie says, "It sounds perfect. But listen, I just found out that my cousin is going through some hard times right now. Her lights have been turned off. She was trying to buy a car but was having some credit problems. I'm not going to tell you what she's driving. I want to help her out by at least buying her a decent car, but she says she has it all under control. I think her pride got in the way, and she didn't want to say anything."

Gordon feels sympathetic toward Diane's situation. "Wow, is there anything I can do to help out? I mean she is taking time out of her busy schedule to help plan our beautiful day and put her own problems aside. I tell you what, once everything is done and over with, let's give her a financial blessing to get her back on her feet and to ease her problems."

Valerie cannot believe her ears. Her man is so generous. She just loves him for being who he is. "Now that sounds like a plan. I hate to see her acting so happy when all along she is hurting on the inside. Thank you for understanding."

"I think more families who are fortunate should help out their loved ones who are less fortunate and struggling. To me, it doesn't make sense for someone to be a millionaire and their family is barely making it."

"That is so true. You are right. I can't wait to surprise her."

After Valerie and Gordon end their call, Valerie goes back into the living room and sees Diane asleep on the couch. Valerie decides not to wake Diane even though there is another bedroom available for Diane to sleep in. She remembers from when they were children that Diane can be cranky when she is aroused from her sleep. Crankier than usual, that is. So, Valerie places a blanket over Diane and quietly goes into her bedroom and closes the door, so she can have a good night sleep herself.

Chapter Twenty-Nine

A few months later…

Monique decides to have a 'me' day, so she is at the Baldwin Hills Mall, splurging and spoiling herself as she shops frivolously, going from one store to the next. Walking out of Macy's with a huge smile spread across her face, she sees a face she has not missed seeing over the last several months. Her smile suddenly turns into a frown. Quickly turning in the other direction, Monique hears a voice calling after her. "Monique! Can I talk to you for a minute?" Monique keeps walking as if though she hasn't heard a word. Catching up to her, Rodney places his hand on her arm and says, "I'm sorry, okay. Everything y'all did to me, I deserved it. I just hope you can find it in your heart to forgive a brotha."

Moving her arm from his grasp, Monique yells, "You were wrong for what you did! You thought you had it going on! You hurt me, but that's okay because it's over now, and after this day, if you see me walking down the street, continue walking by!"

Rodney hears her loud and clear but continues to seek forgiveness. "Monique, I asked the Lord to forgive me for what I did. I have been going to church, and the Lord has been dealing with me in His own way. I know you don't want me. All I ask is that you forgive me. Is it possible?"

Monique finds his words hilarious. "You... Really, you... have been going to church?!" Her words tell him that she does not believe anything he is saying.

Not yielding to her sarcastic retort, Rodney remains humble. "I'm serious! I have. You just don't know how hanging from a billboard can make a brotha start thinking about a different life to lead."

Monique is still not buying into his church act. "That was funny! Bye, Rodney." She begins to walk away.

"But, you haven't told me that you will forgive me. Monique, I'm just trying to make amends. No games! I'm just trying to make it right with you. Who knows, if you forgive me, maybe, just maybe... you might find it in your heart to call me one day... or even go out again."

Monique's laughter turns into anger. She has been waiting for a line to come out his mouth. "Really! Well... That would be a HELL TO THE NO! What were you thinking being with three females? You are lucky I didn't catch anything! Because if you had given me anything, forget about setting you up. My ass would've been on Channel 7 for murder one! I would have most definitely caught a case!"

Still not buying into her anger and refraining from becoming angry himself, Rodney calmly says, "Well, I'm going to let you go." This time, he walks away leaving Monique somewhat surprised.

Yelling after him, Monique says, "That's your best bet!"

As Rodney moves quickly away, seeing people beginning to look in their direction, he walks into Macy's to shield himself. As he makes his way to the shoe section, he begins to think about buying a new pair of kicks. Making his way through the women's section to get over to escalator to go up to the men's department, he sees another familiar face. Not thinking about disturbing anyone, he calls out, "Sharon! Sharon! Hold up for a minute!"

Hearing the familiar voice behind her, Sharon turns around and says with force, "Leave me alone! We don't have anything to talk about! You need Jesus!"

"Well as a matter fact, I found Him."

"You're going to hell, playing like that!"

"I'm not playing. I did."

"Well, you should've found Him a long time ago!"

"Better late than never! Sharon, I don't want anything from you but your forgiveness."

"What?" Sharon says, not believing her ears.

Standing squarely in front of her with an earnest look on his face, Rodney repeats himself. "You don't ever have to talk to me again. All I want is your forgiveness for what I did to you. I'm sorry for everything. Jesus forgave me. Can you?"

"The only reason you want forgiveness is because you got caught! If you ask me, you got off easy!"

"Got off easy? I had to get my stomach pumped after what y'all did. But, that's neither here nor there. All I'm asking is for you to forgive me, and I'll leave. I didn't mean to hurt you, and I'm sorry." Rodney looks at Sharon from head to toe. A smile creeps across his face, and he says, "You know… you look beautiful when you're mad."

Fully expecting him to throw her a line, a look of disgust crosses Sharon's face. "You can save all that for someone else! You will never get any more of this, boo-boo! You're going to learn today!"

Backing down, Rodney says, "I just hope that you can forgive a brotha!" And, he turns and walks away, leaving Sharon fuming.

Rodney decides to leave the mall, knowing his heart is not into shopping. He is happy that he ran into two of the three women he wronged. He is happy to have had an opportunity to at least ask for forgiveness. He understands that he did his part. Now, the rest is up to them. And as they say, all he can do is leave it in God's hands.

Leaving the mall, Rodney sees his gas tank is low, so he pulls into a Shell gas station to fill up. As he is pumping his gas, he sees Janelle pulling in. He can't believe his luck, seeing all three women on the same day. Not waiting for her to get out of her car, he walks over to the gas pump that she has pulled up to. Once she steps out and begins to walk to the pump, she stops. She just stares at him. Calmly, Rodney asks, "Janelle, can I talk to you for a minute, please?"

"Back it up, lizard!"

Rodney immediately lifts his hands in surrender. "Wow… Janelle, just for a second?"

"I'm all talked out." She doesn't bother getting gas. She just turns around and gets back into her car. Rodney walks over to her window and leans down.

"Can I just say one thing?"

Full of rage, Janelle yells, "Don't make me shoot you! Get away from my car." Before he can utter another word, she drives off, almost running over his foot.

He yells after her, "I'm sorry!"

Chapter Thirty

The hotel's courtyard has been beautifully decorated for Gordon and Valerie's big day. The theme includes a tropical decor. Draped along the two inner aisles are long white ribbons with large beautiful white bows. The ribbons are connected to tall clear fish tanks that are positioned at the end of every other row. Each tank is filled with small colorful tropical fish. The fish tanks and ribbon are used to block off the center aisles, forcing people to enter each row by the outside aisles only. This maneuver helps to keep the traffic down and the decorations from being disturbed. The chairs are adorned with satin green chair covers with gold satin ribbons neatly tied to the back.

The altar is beautifully decorated as well. In the very center is an elaborate waterfall that has a rope light secured to the bottom. The light illuminates the water as it sprinkles down. The waterfall is positioned directly behind the altar, which consists of a large white arch that has baby breath intertwined within it and small white Christmas lights that blink off and on. On either side of the arch are two palm trees that have tiny white lights adorning the trunks.

Finally, in the center aisle is a silky white runner. Along both edges are more tiny white lights that twinkle like stars in a midnight sky.

As the adult guests arrive, each one is given a camera that is to be used throughout the wedding and the reception to capture the couples' most memorable wedding moments. The children, on the other hand, are given bubbles to blow, causing the atmosphere to be even more magical.

The long-awaited moment of the wedding ceremony has come. As the tinkle of the organ keys begin to sound, a hush falls over the crowd. "A Ribbon in the Sky" begins to play as Gordon and the preacher enter the courtyard, followed by his best man and the groomsmen. Once the men are positioned near the altar, the song changes to "Endless Love." The bridesmaids enter, followed by the maid of honor, Diane.

The melody switches to instrumental music, as two ushers roll out a royal green runner, which is 100 feet long. Down the middle of the runner is Valerie's name with her future last name printed on it. As the soft music continues to play, two beautiful little flower girls walk down the runner, throwing rose petals as they make their way to the altar. The little girls are beautifully adorned with white dresses that have lace flower petals stitched all over the bottom portion.

Finally, the moment everyone has been waiting for: Valerie's entrance. When the surprise guest singer begins to sing, who has a voice that sounds like the perfect blend of Luther Vandross and Johnny Gill, everyone stands up to greet the bride. Valerie and her father enter the courtyard from the hotel. As she looks around, a smile covers her face. When she sees the courtyard filled with guests, her smile grows brighter. As they walk over to the runner, her father looks at her with a proud look in his eyes. When they reach the beginning of the runner, Valerie looks up and sees Gordon's handsome face that carries a smile that lets everyone know he is experiencing the happiest day of his life. Seeing him makes her smile turn into a grin, showing all of her teeth. She and her father begin their march to the altar. On the way, Valerie whispers, "This is so beautiful."

Once they reach the altar, the preacher asks, "Who gives this young lady away today?" before answering the preacher's question, Valerie's father looks over to his wife, who is seated behind them, then back to the preacher with a smile on his face. He answers, "Her mother and I do."

When Valerie quickly glances at her mother, she can see that her mother is filled with joy. Then, her father lifts her veil, kisses her on the cheek, then he takes his place next to his wife. Gordon then stands in the place where Valerie's father stood. Taking her hand, he whispers, "I love you. You look beautiful."

The next voice that is heard is the preacher. He says, "Love is in the air. If there is anyone here who feels that these two should not be married, let them speak now or forever hold your peace." After a thirty-second pause, the preacher continues. "Well then, the rings please. Gordon, please face Valerie and repeat after me. With this ring, I thee wed." Gordon repeats the words, as he slides a ring on Valerie's finger.

The preacher then says to Valerie, "Valerie, please repeat after me. With this ring, I thee wed."

Valerie says, "With this ring, I thee wed." She slides a wedding band on Gordon's finger.

Finalizing the ceremony, the preacher says, "I now pronounce you husband and wife. You may now kiss your bride."

As Gordon leans in to take Valerie into his arms and kiss her, the guests stand up and applaud. After the kiss that seals their vows, Gordon and Valerie turn and begin to walk down the aisle, as the wedding party follows. The guests are taking pictures, and the children blow bubbles.

The wedding party and the guests make their way over to the ballroom. The tables are elegantly decorated with gold and royal green tablecloths. The tables that have gold tablecloths have chairs covered in royal green, and the tables with the royal green tablecloths have gold-covered chairs. Each table has a beautiful centerpiece consisting of a tall bowl filled with tropical fish. Around the ball is a ring a beautiful tropical flowers. Each place setting consists of a square mirror with a white plate sitting on top of it, complete with a cloth napkin, silverware, and a long-stemmed glass.

The table for the wedding party is formed in an arc circle. The same decor that adorns all of the guest tables is on the wedding party's table as well. Valerie takes in the beautiful decor. She looks over to Diane and says, "This is so beautiful, cousin. I don't know what to say. I had my doubts… I didn't know how this was going to turn out, but I have to say, you did your thang! Thank you so much." She gives Diane a big hug.

"Awe! You are so welcome, but wait until you see your wedding gift that I have for both of you."

"This wedding alone is the best wedding gift you could have ever given us. You outdid yourself, and I'm so happy that the cake came out just the way I wanted it." They both glance over to the wedding cake table. Upon it sits a five-tier cake decorated with tropical colors. In between the five tiers are tropical fish floating around inside beautiful glass bowls.

Diane says, "Oh, you ain't seen nothing yet!"

Once all the guests are seated at their tables, their attention turns to Valerie and Gordon as they sway across the dance floor to their wedding song. Once the dance is over, Valerie and Gordon walk around hand-in-hand and thank their guests for coming. As they make their way back to their seats to consume their delicious-looking meal, they pass a beautiful area that has been sectioned off for guests to place the tons of gifts and cards. After their meal has been consumed and they have danced and danced and danced with various people, Diane walks over and tells them, "It's time to go."

As Gordon is smiling at Valerie, admiring her beauty in her gorgeous gown, Valerie asks, "Time to go where?"

Ignoring her cousin's question, Diane hands Gordon two tickets. Taking the tickets from Diane, Gordon says, "Okay. Thank you. You have done a beautiful job with everything. I truly appreciate it."

Diane responds, "This is my gift to both of you. All expenses paid for a two-week stay, round-trip to Hawaii for your honeymoon. Now, it's time to go." They are both very excited, and they give her a big hug. Then, Gordon's groomsmen take him off for a moment.

While the men are gone, Valerie says to Diane with concern, "Is that why your lights are turned off, so you could buy these tickets?"

"Please! The power of a credit card can do wonders!"

With raised eyebrows, Valerie asks, "Diane, tell me you didn't use that credit card to purchase those tickets."

Diane, acting very nonchalantly, says, "How else was I going to get them? Never mind that. It's time to go now."

When Gordon returns, the three of them walk out to the front of the hotel. Valerie looks around, and in her disappointment, she asks, "No limousine?"

Without answering, Diane walks toward a black Cadillac Escalade, and Valerie and Gordon follow her.

Opening the front door, "Na, limousines are so overrated. Plus with this, you don't have to pay by the hour."

Gordon opens the door for his wife, and once she slides in, he closes the door after her and walks around to the other side and gets in himself. Valerie says, "Oh, my gosh! Diane, you bought us a Cadillac Escalade? You're just full of surprises… But, if you're driving us to the airport, how are you going to get back?"

Looking around the luxurious vehicle, Gordon says, "I want to take you for a long drive in this when we get back."

Diane says, "I'm just giving y'all a ride!"

Valerie smiles at Gordon, then she turns her head toward Diane. She is smiling while shaking her head, trying to play it off. She has a bad feeling about how Diane got the Escalade.

While Gordon is preoccupied, Valerie leans over to Diane and whispers, "Tell me you didn't, Diane." Diane brushes her cousin off by saying, "We don't have time for small talk. Now, go and have a beautiful honeymoon. I'll be back to pick y'all up in two weeks."

Chapter Thirty-One

Rodney is at work at LAX on the loading docks. As he grabs a suitcase and lifts it to toss it into the cart, he hears a muffled sound. At first, he ignores it and lifts another suitcase and places it into the cart. The sound is a little louder now, so Rodney steps away from the luggage and begins to search out the location the sound is coming from. Noticing that it is coming from overhead, Rodney lifts his head up toward a billboard. Low and behold, a guy is hanging from it. Rodney shakes his head and says to himself, "I wonder who he did wrong. Been there done that, brotha!" Because he feels bad for the guy, he calls 911 emergency services to have the Fire Department come and take the man down.

On other side of town, Janelle is at home in her bedroom, watching television. She picks up the phone and dials Monique's number, who is at home washing dishes.

Monique answers, "Hello?"

Bypassing a greeting, Janelle says, "Girl, I had to string up another one!"

"Janelle, what are you talking about?"

"I was talking to this guy and found out he was messing around with someone else! Up on the billboard, he went!"

Monique begins to laugh. "Girl, you are crazy!"

Janelle laughs a little herself and says, "I'm tired of these men! Why is it that they have to be with more than one female at a time?"

"All men aren't like that. Plus, when you find out they are messing around, you know you're not working with the man. You are working with a boy!"

"You got all that right! Guess what. I saw that fool Rodney at the gas station!"

"You did? What happened?"

Janelle sits up on her bed, so she can explain to Monique about the brief encounter she had with Rodney. "Nothing! I told him to get away from my car. As I was driving off, he hollered something out, but I didn't hear him. I didn't want to know. I didn't care one bit!"

Monique has moved from the kitchen into her dining room. She opens up a jigsaw puzzle and begins to work on it. Then casually, she says, "I saw him, too. Want to hear something crazy?"

"What?" Janelle asks.

"Well, he said he found Jesus or something. He kept apologizing for what he did." She picks up the remote and starts flipping through channels, trying to see if she can find something decent to watch on TV, pushing the puzzle to the side.

"Do you believe him?"

"No, not really, but it doesn't make a difference. I'm just glad I'm not with that fool any longer!"

"At least this time when I was talking to this other idiot, I didn't take me long to find out that he was with somebody else! I think I am going to write a book called *What To Do with Your Man When You Catch Him Cheating* and a list of stuff to do to him."

Hearing the anger building in Janelle's Voice, Monique says, "Girl, did I tell you there are places you can go for help? Oh, hold on. Someone is calling." Monique clicks to her other line and says, "Hello."

Sharon, who is sitting in her car at the beach, says, "Girl, I don't believe this!"

Monique can hear that something is wrong with Sharon, so she asks, "What's wrong?"

Sharon says, "I'm pregnant!"

"Pregnant! By whom? Wait, hold on for a minute!" She clicks the phone back over. "Janelle, Sharon is on the other line. Let me call you right back." Switching the line back over, Monique continues her conversation with Sharon. "Sharon, I'm back. That was Janelle on the other line. Now, what are you talking about?"

"I'm pregnant by Rodney. I don't know how because I just had my cycle, but I kept having other symptoms as well. I went to my doctor, and she told me that in some cases, even though you have a cycle, you can still get pregnant, but eventually my cycle will stop."

"So, what are you going to do?'

"I don't want it! By him, hell no. I'm getting rid of it," Sharon exclaims.

Monique objects. "Don't take it out on the baby. The way you get even with him is to make him pay for every-thing. And, I mean everything. Child support, diapers, bottles, Gerber's food. I'm talking about preschool fund, elementary, high school, and college. You hear me? I'm talking the whole nine yards. Did I mention clothes, doctor's visits, transportation, and a top of the line baby stroller?"

Sharon smiles. But apprehension fills her, and she asks, "What if he doesn't want it?"

Monique answers assuredly, "He doesn't have a choice in this matter. If he trips out about it, we will turn his world upside down. When I was talking to Janelle just now, she told me she had to hang another guy up on the billboard because she found out he was cheating on her."

Sharon laughs a little and says, "What? That girl is crazy for real." She pauses, then asks, "Monique, why aren't you tripping about this?"

"I'm fine. Girl, I'm a grown woman. Plus, there are lots of other men out here besides him. This is not about me right now. It's about the baby inside of you. Don't you dare get rid of it because of him!"

Sharon feels so much better and is thankful that she made the call to Monique. "You are real cool, girl. Sorry, we had to meet under the circumstances that we did."

Chapter Thirty-Two

In a hotel suite in Hawaii, Gordon and Valerie are enjoying the beginning of their honeymoon vacation. Gordon looks over to his wife and says, "Wow, what a day we had. Everything went perfectly."

Valerie responds, "Honey, I love you so much."

"I love you too, Mrs. Benson."

Standing up to go into the restroom, Valerie says, "Give me a minute, honey." When she comes from the bathroom she looks at Gordon with a little sadness on her face and says, "Well, I hope you love me in the next five days because we're going to have to wait." He looks at her, not immediately catching on to what she is referring to.

"Five days? Have to wait... Oh, that. It's okay, baby. I love you so much make it six days, just to make sure. Your cousin really did a great job with our wedding. She really loves you a lot. And for her to go all out to buy an SUV for our big day, so we can go out in style, that's probably why she is struggling."

All of a sudden, a feeling of nervousness moves around in Valerie's stomach. "Ummm... honey. You said that you love me right?"

Gordon smiles as he looks at her and says, "Always. I'm never going to let you go again. We're going to have lots of babies and grow old together."

Valerie takes a deep breath and trusts her gut that honesty is the best policy. "I have something to tell you."

Gordon can tell she is serious. He places his hands on her shoulders and looks her in the eyes and asks, "What is it, baby? You can tell me anything."

"Anything?"

"Yeah, anything."

"Well… my cousin, sorta bought that Escalade with your credit card. I'm so sorry. I didn't know she would do something like that."

Gordon is concerned but attempts to keep his shock under control. "I'm just curious, but what was she driving before?"

"Well… I don't know how to tell you. But, it was a golf cart."

Gordon's shock turns to humor, as he tries to hold back a laugh. "Did you say a golf cart?"

"Yeah… That's why I was hesitant to say anything."

"Oh my! She needs that Escalade. You know what, I'm not mad. You know, baby, this is our honeymoon, and it's all good. I do have to ask though, did you get the credit card back from her?"

"Oh, my gosh!"

"What?"

"I got so caught up in the moment. She still has it! I never got it back from her! Where is my purse? I'll call her now." Valerie's anxiety has turned to frantic energy.

Gordon pulls her slowly by her arms into an embrace and whispers into her ear. "Calm down. It's okay. Just tell her not to use it for anything else! That's all."

Valerie nods her head to Gordon, as she dials Diane's number. Diane does not answer. The phone just rings.

Back in California, Diane is making a call of her own. Once again, she is calling the electric company. When an operator answers, she says, "Yes, I'm calling to have my lights turned back on!" After Diane makes her call, she puts the phone down. She doesn't see the missed call from Valerie until the next morning. She immediately calls back.

Valerie answers the phone, "Hello?"

Diane has no idea why her cousin is calling when she should be enjoying her honeymoon. As the phone rings, in a frantic voice, Diane asks herself, "Oh, my goodness. Is the honeymoon over already?" When Valerie picks up, Diana says, "Hello, Valerie? What's going on? Sorry, I didn't get back to you last night. Wait, you're supposed be on your honeymoon. Don't tell me it's over already. I have a question for you."

"First of all, no, the honeymoon is not over, crazy. What is your question?"

"Just to let you know, I used the card to have my lights turned back on. But, what is the limit on the credit card because they're a lot more things I need to get?"

"There is no limit left for you. Your limit has been met! That's why I was calling you to let you know not to use that card any longer! You don't need anything else! Girl, you bought an Escalade, and now you're using it to have your lights turned back on!"

"Oh, Lord!" Gordon says in the background.

Meanwhile, Diane is putting her shoes on. "Can I at least get some gas?"

"Hold on. Honey, this crazy girl wants to know if she can get some gas."

Gordon is blown away by the forwardness of Diane. Shaking his head in disgust, he replies, "Tell her that she can buy some gas. Then, cut up that card!"

To Diane, Valerie says, "Yeah, get the gas. But after that, cut up that card!"

Diane begins to do a little dance. "Tell him thanks. Oh and, Valerie?"

"Yeah?"

"Don't tell him that I'm filling it up!"

"I believe he has that feeling already. Bye, Missy." As she hangs up the phone with her cousin, she blows her husband a kiss.

Chapter Thirty-Three

Sharon has finally wrapped her mind around the fact that she is pregnant by Rodney. Beginning to feel some happiness about the situation, she decides to go to her mother's house and share her news. Unlocking the front door, Sharon walks in and calls out to her mother. "Mama? Where are you?" Sharon can hear some sounds coming from the kitchen, and then she hears her mother's voice.

"I'm in the kitchen, baby." As Sharon reaches the kitchen, she sees her mother standing next to the stove with bell peppers and onions on the cutting board. Her mother is chopping them up, as she prepares dinner. Sharon leans over and gives her mother a quick kiss on the cheek.

"Guess what, Mama? I have a surprise for you."

"I'm too old to be guessing. What is it, child?"

"You're about to be a grandma again!"

Sharon doesn't get the response she is expecting. "Pregnant! By who? I know you're not talking about that boy… What's his name…? Roger Rabbit?"

"Rodney, Ma. He is a rabbit though."

"Okay now, having a baby is not easy! I'm already raising your sister's child now."

Right at that moment, Sharon's niece Angie yells from the bathroom. "Grandma! Grandma!"

Sharon's mother yells back, "Yes, dear?"

"I think I've been shot."

Sharon's mother drops the knife, and they both take off towards the bathroom. They find Angie in the hallway holding her stomach. Angie looks up and sees her aunt. "Hi, auntie. Call the police because somebody's going down for this one!" she says, continuing to hold her stomach.

Sharon's mother is totally confused about what is going on. "But, I haven't heard any gunshots!"

In a serious tone, Angie says, "I just came out of the bathroom, and it doesn't look good! Call the FBI, Grandma. Call the CIA. We need justice. I feel like my stomach is in knots. What's wrong with me?"

They look around the bathroom; then, they look at each other. They figure out what is going on. With a smile on her face, Sharon's mother says, "Baby, you have been shot by your young lady-hood. Let me tell you all about it."

Back in the kitchen, Sharon's mother rinses her hands. Wanting to give them some privacy and to be a bit of help, Sharon says, "I will be back."

Angie asked, "Where are you going? You just got here."

"I'm going to the store to buy you a gift that is going to last you for a week." Sharon smiles because she knows her niece has no idea what she is referring to.

"A whole week? I like gifts, but right now Grandma and I are about to take somebody down because this don't make no sense! Grandma, why haven't you called 911 yet?"

"Baby girl, what's going on with you doesn't call for 911. What you are feeling is called cramps! You are now at the beginning stages of your young lady-hood."

"If I have to feel like this, I don't like young lady-hood. Can I wait until five or six years from now and try this again?"

Sharon's mother burst into laughter at her grand-daughter's question. "Baby… time doesn't wait for anyone, and your time for this is now. It's going to be alright. You're going to be just fine." Angie looks at her grandmother with disbelieving eyes. She shrugs her shoulders and lowers her head.

Chapter Thirty-Four

Having spent the entire morning in the hotel room, Gordon and Valerie have finally gotten dressed and are prepared to head out to have a bite to eat for lunch. Gordon is still thinking about Diane spending money on his credit card as if though it is hers. He looks at his wife and asks, "Do you think she will really cut that card up?"

"To tell you the truth, I don't know! I don't think Diane ever had a credit card with unlimited use!"

Back in California, Diane is still up to her tricks. At the gas station, the attendant asks her, "Can I help you?"

She says to the attendant, "I would like to put $5,000 down for credit toward future gas purchases." Without any questions, he rings up the purchase. She takes the receipt and says, "Thank you!" From there, she goes to AutoZone and asked to see tires that will fit the Escalade. She makes the purchase and move on down the street to Jiffy Lube. At the counter, she says, "I would like to get $1,500 worth of credit for future tune-ups."

Back in Hawaii, Gordon says, "But, next time I give you a credit card, please don't tell your cousin about it. Okay?"

Looking her husband in the eyes, Valerie answers, "I promise."

Then, Valerie's phone rings. "Hello."

On the other line, Diane says, "I'm through now. I'm cutting up the card."

"You did just buy gas, right?"

"I think we have a party line."

"These are cell phones, crazy. You don't get party lines."

"Me a speaks no English. Wrong numba! I'll talk to you later, bye." Diane disconnect the phone, leaving Valerie hanging.

Gordon looks at Valerie and asks, "So, did she just get some gas?"

"I really hope so, but the only way to know for sure is when you get the statement."

Gordon laughs half-heartedly. "Oh, that's a scary thought, but enough about your cousin. We have a whole two weeks here in Hawaii. What would you like to do first?"

"How about after lunch we take a tour of these beautiful islands and then play it by ear from there?"

"Sounds good to me," Gordon says and leans over and kisses his wife.

Epilogue

Two months later…

Valerie tells Gordon she's pregnant. A few months after that, she learns her baby is actually twins. Gordon is so thrilled and excited about the prospect of growing his family. After much discussion, Valerie takes a leave of absence from her job and focuses her attention on preparing the nursery and having a safe and healthy delivery in five months.

When Gordon and Valerie first returned from their honeymoon, they had Diane return the Escalade, and they bought her a Honda Civic. At first, she was upset, but deep down she knew she was wrong. She thanked them for the car. Later, Diane ended up dating one of Gordon's grooms- men. When Gordon learned about it, he was hesitant to say anything at first. But, he finally decided to share with his friend that she's a good person, but he warned him about giving her a credit card.

Monique, Sharon, and Janelle ended up going their separate ways until a dramatic situation bought them back together again. And of course, Rodney was the major factor. He tried to return to his old ways, but the ladies shut him down with the quickness.

Cramps

Even though it was explained to Sharon's niece that she's going to have cycles every month and how to take care of it when it comes, she doesn't like experiencing the physical aspects of the pain that comes from **CRAMPS**!

About the Author

La Noyce Taylor was born and raised in Los Angeles. Growing up as a little girl, she loved to be in plays and things of that nature. As a teenager, she enrolled in Drama class at her middle and high schools to continue her passion. As an adult, she tried out for stand-up comedy at her church and for a comic show. She also took a chance in a small business doing Open Mic Nights (Talent Shows). From there, she went on and made a commercial. Then, she wrote a movie script believing that her vision would also come to life. It has been a long journey for her, and now that she has arrived, there is no turning back.

www.ingramcontent.com/pod-product-compliance
Lightning Source LLC
Chambersburg PA
CBHW070825250626
47170CB00006B/2214